GANGSTA
GRANNY
STRIKES AGAIN!

For my wonderful mum,

who is also a Gangsta Granny

THANK-YOUS

MASTERS OF DISGUISE:

ANN-JANINE MURTAGH
My Executive Publisher

CHARLIE REDMAYNE
CEO

TONY ROSS
My Illustrator

PAUL STEVENS
My Literary Agent

HARRIET WILSON
My Editor

KATE BURNS
Art Editor

SAMANTHA STEWART
Publishing Manager

VAL BRATHWAITE
Creative Director

ELORINE GRANT
Art Director

KATE CLARKE
Art Director

MATTHEW KELLY
Art Director

SALLY GRIFFIN
Designer

GERALDINE STROUD
My PR Director

TANYA HOUGHAM
Audio Producer

David Walliams

It has been a year since Ben lost his beloved Gangsta Granny, but the legend of The Black Cat lives on!

MEET THE
CHARACTERS
IN THE STORY

BEN

Our hero is an ordinary twelve-year-old boy, who has had
the most extraordinary adventure. With the help of his
granny, in her guise as The Black Cat, he very nearly stole
the Crown Jewels from the Tower of London. However,
his days as an international jewel thief are over. Ben is now
focusing on his big dream: to become a plumber.

MUM

By day, Linda works at a
nail salon. By night, she is a
ballroom-dancing superfan.
Her favourite TV show ever is
Strictly Stars Dancing. There is
one professional dancer she loves
above all the rest. His name is
Flavio Flavioli and the family
home has become a shrine to him.
Linda is desperate for her only
child, Ben, to forget his plumbing
dream and become a ballroom
champion just like Flavio.

DAD

Dad works as a security guard
at the local supermarket. Pete
is not a fast runner – in the past
ten years he has only caught
one shoplifter, and that was an
old man on a Zimmer frame
who was escaping with tubs of
margarine – but he too loves
ballroom dancing. He caught
the ballroom bug from his wife,
and now the couple rehearse
routines all over the house.

RAJ

Raj is the most loved store owner in town. He runs the famously messy Raj's News, but everyone stops by to enjoy his crazy deals and out-of-date sweets. Raj has always been a good friend to Ben – they became closer when Ben lost his granny, and Raj is always there to cheer the boy up with a silly joke or some free chocolate.

MR PARKER

Mr Parker is a nosy neighbour. He is a retired major and now runs the local Neighbourhood Watch group, Lower Toddle branch. It is a collection of oldies who have joined forces to keep an eye out for burglars, but Mr Parker uses it as an excuse to spy on everyone. One person he has got his eye on particularly is Ben. The nosy neighbour had been convinced the boy and his granny had stolen the Crown Jewels, but nobody had believed him. Now Mr Parker is out for revenge!

FLAVIO FLAVIOLI

Flavio is the heart-throb of the wildly popular TV show *Strictly Stars Dancing*. The Italian king of the dance floor has a deep-mahogany spray tan, shiny slicked-back hair and the most dazzlingly white teeth you ever did see. He wears brightly coloured all-in-one dance outfits, and so he looks like a boiled sweet in a wrapper.

EDNA

Ben met Edna at Granny's funeral. She is Granny's cousin. Edna took a shine to Ben, and over the past year they have become friends. The boy pops round every Sunday to Edna's old folk's home for tea and cake, a game of Scrabble and a natter about the olden days.

THE LIBRARIAN

This lady has worked at the library all her life. She is suspicious about Ben, and whenever he visits the library she has her beady eyes on him.

THE QUEEN

The Queen needs no introduction. She met Ben
and his granny the night they tried to steal HER
Crown Jewels from the Tower of London. The
Queen was so touched by their special bond that
she pardoned the pair on the spot.

BUTLER THE BUTLER

Mr Butler is the conveniently
named butler at Buckingham
Palace. Impossibly old, he has
loyally served the Queen ever
since she was a little girl.

PC FUDGE

Ben and Granny met PC
Fudge on the way to steal
the Crown Jewels. The
policeman stopped them
when Granny drove her
mobility scooter on the
motorway. They managed
to fool him, and he ended
up giving them a lift to the
Tower of London!

MILLICENT

Granny left her mobility scooter to Ben
in her will, as she knew he loved it so
much. Now he keeps it in the garage.

THE BLACK CAT

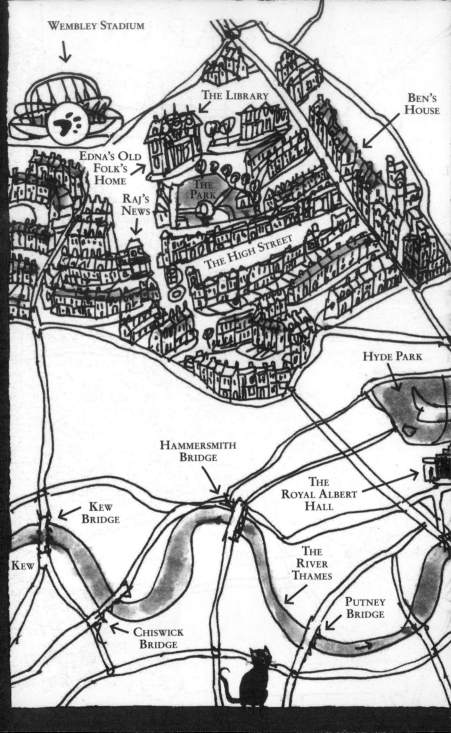

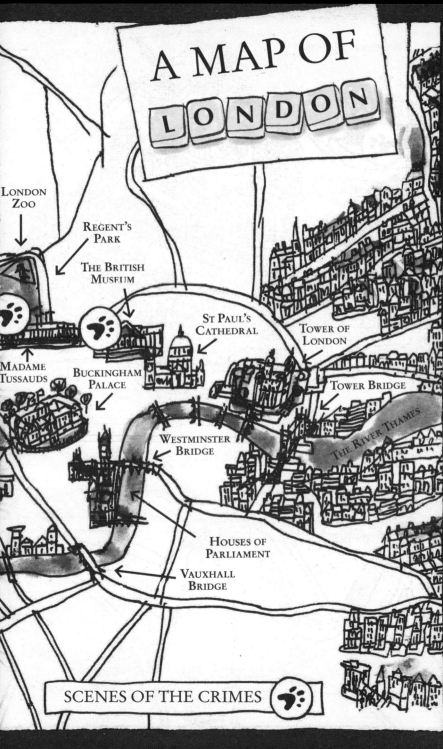

PART ONE

RETURN
OF THE
CAT

1

A BEAUTIFUL BOUQUET OF CABBAGES

"**Cabbages?**" came a voice from behind Ben.

The boy was standing by his granny's headstone in the churchyard. It had been a year since her passing, and Ben was placing a beautiful bouquet of **cabbages** there as a tribute.

Ben turned round. It was a familiar face. Edna, a cousin of Granny's. He'd met her at the funeral last Christmas time and they had struck up something of a friendship. Now, once a week, Ben popped round to her old folk's home to have a chat, often about Granny, and to help with any plumbing problems, which made him super popular with everyone there.

Thick glasses that make her eyes go all googly

Mop of grey hair

Hearing aid that whistles so loudly it makes everyone around her become deaf

Kindly face

False teeth

Pink cardigan

Used tissue tucked up sleeve

Floral-print dress

Bag of boiled sweets in handbag

Odour of Lavender foot cream

Tan tights

Shopper even when not going shopping

Sensible shoes

Edna was your textbook old lady.

"Oh, hello, Edna," replied Ben. "What are you doing here?"

The old lady was holding a single red rose and wearing a sad smile.

"Oh! You see, dear, I come here once a week to lay a rose on my late husband's resting place. Why do you have a bouquet of **cabbages**?"

"For Granny. She loved them so much."

Edna looked wistful. "Oh yes. I do remember the sound they made whenever she came over for tea."

"**Cabbages** don't talk!"

"No. I mean the sound of your granny's bottom whoopsies after she'd eaten one. Like…"

"A duck quacking!" exclaimed Ben.

"I couldn't have put it better, dear!"

"QUACK! QUACK! QUACK!" he mimicked, trundling along the path, letting out a little quack with each step.

The pair burst out laughing.

"HA! HA!"

A tear traced a path down his cheek. Ben wasn't sure if it was a happy tear or a sad tear. Most likely it was a bit of both. Granny's passing had hit Ben the hardest.

Despite the age gap, they were closer than anyone in the family. When she died, Ben felt as if the world would stop turning. But it didn't. It just carried on as normal. Ben had everyday things to do, like:

brush his teeth…

go to school…

take a bath…

do his homework…

and read **PLUMBING WEEKLY**.

But he always felt the loss. With Granny gone, it was as if a part of him were missing.

"I don't know why I'm crying," he said, sniffing.

Edna pulled her used tissue from her sleeve and dabbed Ben's face with it.

"Because you loved her. Feeling sad is the price you pay for love. And, ooh goodness me, you were the apple of her eye! She adored you, Ben. Never stopped talking about you!"

The boy gazed up to the sky. "Is Granny looking down on us now?"

"I'm sure she is," replied Edna. "With great pride,

I imagine, at what a kind young man you are growing up to be – looking after me and my plumbing so well."

"Granny was a very special lady. She wasn't your average grandma. She was my…"

Ben hesitated. He was about to say **"Gangsta Granny"**!

"Your what, dear?" asked Edna.

"Nothing," muttered Ben. He needed to keep Granny's secrets secret. Even from her best friend, Edna. No one else knew about Granny's double life as an international jewel thief, going under the name of **THE BLACK CAT**. Well, no one else other than *Her Majesty the Queen,* who discovered them trying to steal her *Crown Jewels* that fateful night at the Tower of London.

"You were about to tell me something, dear…"

"Maybe one day," replied Ben. "I'll pop round and see you on Sunday, normal time."

"I'll get the SCRABBLE out! And don't forget the **Murray Mints!**"

"I won't!"

As Ben walked out of the graveyard, Edna smiled and waved goodbye. Then she laid the single red rose down on her late husband's grave.

At that moment, Ben spotted a **black cat** slinking out from behind Granny's headstone.

It moved like a panther. The cat turned, looked straight at the boy and miaowed.

"MIAOW!"

Ben doubled back to stroke the cat, but as quickly as it had appeared it disappeared. It leaped up on to the stone wall that circled the graveyard.

Then with one more spring
the creature
was gone.

2

DING!

The bell on the door rang as Ben waltzed into the newsagent's shop.

"Ah! Ben! My favourite customer!" announced the jolly man behind the counter. Raj was like a giant Jelly Baby, forever smiling and with a light dusting of sugar.

"Hi, Raj!" replied Ben. "Have you got the new **PLUMBING WEEKLY?**"

"Never mind about U-bends and cisterns and stopcocks!" he exclaimed. "Have you not seen the news?"

"What news?"

"The news news!"

"What news news?"

"The news news news!"

"What news news news?"

"The mask of Tutankhamun has been –" Raj left a dramatic pause – "stolen!"

It was all there on the front page of the newspaper.

THE BIGGEST
HEIST
IN HISTORY!

The death mask of King Tutankhamun has been stolen. Recently restored, it was on loan from the Museum of Egyptian Antiquities in Cairo and had been put on display in the British Museum in London. Last night, the death mask went missing in what is believed to be the greatest theft the world has ever known. That is because the mask is absolutely priceless. It dates back more than 3,000 years to when it was placed in the tomb of the Ancient Egyptian boy-king Tutankhamun. The large and heavy gold mask is adorned with precious stones. It was made for the pharaoh to take with him to the afterlife when he died at the age of just 18. The death mask is one of the most famous objects in the world, and as such is impossible to value.

"That mask must be worth millions!" exclaimed Ben.

"Billions!"

"Trillions?"

"Squillions!"

"Are squillions a real amount?" asked Ben.

"I am not sure. But gazillions are."

DING! went the bell on the door again. Immediately, the pair looked over and saw that the door was open, but there was no one there.

"Who was that?" hissed Ben.

"No one," replied Raj.

"It can't have been no one."

"I didn't see anyone come in or out."

"Who was it, then?"

"A freak gust of wind," said Raj, walking over to the door and closing it.

Meanwhile, Ben scanned the aisles of the shop, but he couldn't spot anyone.

He lowered his voice. "So, who stole Tutankhamun's mask?"

"No one knows. But the thief was so daring that they even left behind a clue."

"What kind of clue?"

"According to the radio, the thief spelled out a clue in SCRABBLE letters at the scene of the crime."

The boy's eyes widened. SCRABBLE had always been his grandma's favourite game.

"What did the SCRABBLE letters say?"

"MIAOW."

"Miaow?"

"Miaow! Like cats go – MIAOW!"

Ben was stunned into silence. It sounded awfully like it was a clue to the identity of the thief.

"Are you all right, Ben?" asked Raj.

"I'm fine," he lied.

"You look faint!" Raj began running around his shop. "Here, have a sniff of an **extra-strong mint**. That will bring you round!"

The man all but inserted the packet up the boy's nose, and Ben took a long, minty snort.

"It's impossible," muttered Ben.

"What's impossible?"

"It can't be true!"

"It is true! Look! It's all over the TV as well!"

With that, Raj thumped the little black-and-white television he kept on a shelf behind the counter. A newsflash flickered into view.

The newsreader announced, "We bring you some breaking news. There has been a dramatic development. The mask of Tutankhamun is –"

"Oh, my word! They must have found it!" exclaimed Raj.

"– still missing…"

"I don't know why they bother," muttered Raj, turning off the television.

Ben was lost in thought. The theft of a priceless artefact from a heavily guarded museum had the pawprints of **THE BLACK CAT** all over it. Who else other than a legendary international jewel thief could pull off such a daring heist? The SCRABBLE letters even spelled out M I A O W. That was not a clue. It was a taunt that was telling the police, "You can't catch me!"

But, and it was a BIG BUT,* the thief couldn't be his Gangsta Granny. She had been gone for a year.

This was a GIANT PUZZLE Ben desperately wanted to solve.

"Ben, do you remember a year ago there were all those priceless jewels left outside that charity shop?" asked Raj.

"In the biscuit tin! Of course I remember," replied the boy.

They were the jewels he'd found one night in Granny's kitchen. A discovery that had kick-started the whole adventure!

Granny had sworn that they were all worthless costume jewels, that she hadn't been **THE BLACK CAT** after all.

But it had been a DOUBLE BLUFF!

The jewels turned out to be worth millions. All the money went to help old people. Granny really had been a proper **GANGSTA!**

"There were rumours flying around town that the jewels must have come from the haul of a world-

---

* Not a BIG BUTT. That is something entirely different and has no place in a children's book.

famous thief!" said Raj. "A thief who no one knew the name of!"

"Not that famous, then."

"All right, Clever Clog!"

"It's Clogs!"

"No more special offers for you!"

"The theft of King Tutankhamun's mask couldn't have been the work of the same thief, though."

"And how do you know that?" came a voice from behind Ben.

The boy spun round in horror. Now he was nose to nose with his nosy nemesis.

"Mr Parker!"

he exclaimed.

3

PUDDLE

OF

TROUBLE

Mr Parker was the nosiest nosy parker there ever was. He was a retired army major, and now ran the local **Neighbourhood Watch** group, Lower Toddle branch. This was a collection of people who kept an eye out for burglars. But Mr Parker took it one step further. He spied on absolutely everyone.

Mr Parker had very nearly landed Ben and his granny in a puddle of trouble when they'd tried to steal the *Crown Jewels*. That night, Mr Parker had ended up humiliated by the policemen who hadn't believed his story. Ben and Granny had walked free, but Mr Parker had held a GIANT GRUDGE against the boy ever since. He was determined to one day finally see Ben unveiled as a criminal mastermind.

"I *said*," began the nosy neighbour in his nasal voice, "how do you know so much about the theft of Tutankhamun's mask?"

"Erm," spluttered Ben. "I don't know anything!"

"You just said you did!"

"Did I?"

"YES!"

"Ah, Mr Parker!" began Raj, staring back at the man. "My least favourite customer!"

Mr Parker was sporting his usual pork-pie hat, rain mac and highly polished brown brogue shoes. At Raj's greeting his sour face SOURED some more.

"Hmm," said Mr Parker. It was unclear what this meant, but it sounded disapproving. "I should report you!"

"Whatever for?" asked the newsagent.

"Selling out-of-date chocolate bars!" declared Mr Parker, brandishing one he'd picked up from the counter.

"Let me see that!" snapped Raj, snatching the bar out of the man's hands.

The newsagent studied the wrapper. "It is only ten years out of date! It is perfectly fine to eat!"

A sinister smile spread across Parker's face. "Well, you eat it, then, Mr Raj!"

"*Me?*"

"Yes! You!"

Raj shot a panicked look over at Ben. He needed help. The boy shrugged. Raj shook his head and unwrapped the bar.

"It is so old that the chocolate has turned white!" exclaimed Mr Parker.

"It is meant to be white," lied Raj. "It is white chocolate."

"It says 'dark chocolate' on the wrapper," added Ben innocently.

"You are not helping, Ben!" said Raj, who nibbled the edge of the mouldy chocolate bar.

"Does old chocolate turn white just like old cat poo?" asked Ben.

"Now you are *really* not helping!"

"EAT IT!" ordered Mr Parker.

Poor Raj had tears in his eyes as he munched his way through the dry and dusty snack that had died many years ago. As he did so, against all odds, he began to enjoy the tangy taste. "Mmm. It's actually delicious! Excellent vintage! Please, have a bite!"

This hurled Mr Parker into a rage. "Never mind about that! Ben, you need to tell me everything you know about last night's heist. Because the theft of Tutankhamun's mask has all the hallmarks of one of the crimes of the silver-haired menace: your grandmother! Or, should I say, of her... ACCOMPLICE!"

Ben gulped guiltily. "I don't know what you mean."

"You know exactly what I mean, Benjamin Herbert."

Raj popped his hand in the air. "I have no idea what either of you mean!"

Mr Parker's red eyes narrowed. "So, you little worm," he said, addressing Ben. "Where were you last night?"

"In my bathroom at home fixing the toilet flush!" spluttered Ben.

"Fixing the toilet flush! What twaddle!"

"It's not twaddle. It's true!"

"Have you got an alibi?"

"A what?"

"Someone who can vouch for your whereabouts!" thundered Mr Parker.

"Only the toilet. And toilets can't talk."

"Mine does!" chipped in Raj. "Just last night I could swear it called out in pain when I sat on it!"

"A daring robbery in the dead of night by a figure dressed only in black," continued Mr Parker, pointing at a picture from the grainy security footage at the museum, which was on the front page of the newspapers.

"I don't wear black!" protested Ben.

"You and your grandmother were wearing all black the night I apprehended you!"

"Apart from that one night, I don't!"

Mr Parker looked Ben up and down. "Right now,

you have black socks on!"

"One of them is navy."

"You might be wearing black undercrackers!"

"My undercrackers are brown, actually!" replied Ben.

"Very wise," muttered Raj. "I do the same. In case of a boomtastic* bottom banger!"

"Never mind about bottom bangers! Let me tell you this, young man…" said Mr Parker, leaning in so he could stare right into Ben's eyes, "I have my eye on you!"

Not breaking his gaze, he began stalking away theatrically. Because he wasn't looking where he was going, Mr Parker backed straight into a carousel of cards.

DOINK!

He slipped over.

SLOOSH!

The greetings cards fluttered into the air like butterflies…

WHOOMPH!

…landing on top of him in a shower.

---

* A real word you will find in your **Walliamsictionary**, the finest book of made-up words in the world. The definition of "boomtastic" is "thunderous".

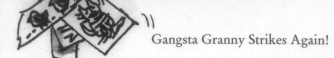

"Ouch! My bottom!" cried Mr Parker from the floor.

A Get Well Soon card landed on his face.

"Looks like I won't need to send you a card!" joked Ben.

"The greetings cards are on special offer!" added Raj. "One hundred and thirty-seven cards for the price of one hundred and thirty-six!"

"HELP ME UP, YOU FOOLS!" thundered Mr Parker.

Ben and Raj hoisted the man up by his armpits.

"OOF!" exclaimed Mr Parker as he landed back on his feet. "Now unhand me, you brutes!"

Ben and Raj shared a confused look. The pair had no idea why they were now "brutes", but they let go of Mr Parker.

"You lied your way out of it last time! This time you won't be so lucky!" he said as he swept out of the shop.

DING!

As Raj righted the carousel, Ben began stuffing the cards back on the shelves.

"What was all that about?" asked Raj.

"I have absolutely no idea," lied Ben.

"Come now! This is your Uncle Raj. You don't need to keep secrets from me."

"I don't have any secrets!"

"We all have secrets! Was it something about your grandma?"

"No!" replied Ben, a little too quickly to be believed. "I have to get home. My mum and dad will be worried."

"Yes. You run along. Would you like to take the **Ballroom Monthly** for your mother? She orders it in. This month it has Flavio on the cover!"

There was indeed a photo of the smug-looking **STRICTLY STARS DANCING** dancer blowing a kiss to the reader.

"Oh! Not him again," muttered Ben. "Yep, I can take it for her."

Raj scoured his famously messy shop before he finally found one. **"Ballroom Monthly? Ballroom Monthly? Ballroom Monthly?** Ah! There it is! In the freezer! Of course! Nice and fresh for you!"

With that, he handed Ben the magazine, which was so cold a white mist danced across it.

WHIZZLE!

Ben slipped the frozen magazine inside his **PLUMBING WEEKLY**. He didn't want anyone to think he read **Ballroom Monthly!** He loved ballcocks, not glitter balls! He put the money down on the counter.

"There you go, Raj!"

"My white-chocolate bars are on special offer."

"No thanks, Raj. I don't like white chocolate!"

"Let me have a peek," said Raj, unwrapping a white-chocolate bar from the counter. "This one is only twenty years out of date. And – oh look – you're in luck! The white chocolate has actually turned brown!"

Ben did not want to risk it. "I'm good, thanks, Raj!"

"Oh! The kids of today are so fussy!" The newsagent took a bite out of the musty white-chocolate bar. **"Delicious!** I know what I'll do – I'll put the white-chocolate bars that have gone brown in the dark-chocolate wrappers, and the dark-chocolate bars that have gone white in the white-chocolate wrappers. I'm a genius!"

"Remind me never to buy chocolate here again!"

"One more special offer?"

"What now?" asked Ben wearily.

"I have some fancy-dress outfits left over from Halloween!"

"No thanks, Raj."

"Ben, haven't you always wanted to dress up as a pretty little princess?"

"NO!" replied the boy firmly.

"Oh! I have! Or how about a lobster?"

Raj did indeed have a large red lobster costume on sale.

"Funnily enough, no!" was Ben's answer.

"Buy nine lobster costumes, get a tenth free!"

"Goodbye, Raj!"

"Goodbye!" chirped the newsagent. "You just missed the deal of the century!"

DING!

4

A GALLOPING POSTBOX

Outside the shop, just next to Raj's red Reliant Robin (an old banger he'd named "the *RAJ RACER*"), Ben spotted something strange. There was a postbox on the street. The strange part was that he was sure it hadn't been there when he'd gone into the shop. Ben quickly dismissed the thought – postboxes don't just appear in minutes – and started walking home. However, when he turned his back, he was sure the postbox had moved. Ben picked up his pace, and then turned round suddenly. The postbox was following him. Now Ben was running. When he looked back, he saw that the postbox was running too! He was being chased by a galloping postbox!

Looking down, he noticed a pair of highly polished brown brogues sticking out from under the postbox. He'd know those shoes anywhere... It was Mr Parker! The nosy parker was following him!

Ben was not the fastest runner and tended to walk the school cross-country runs, often crossing the finishing line the next day. However, with some extra effort, he found he could just about outrun a pensioner disguised as a postbox. Ben sprinted as fast as he could. He took a shortcut across the park and darted through the playground. It was dark and the park keeper was locking up for the night.

"PARK'S CLOSED!" he shouted after Ben, but the boy just kept running.

The postbox was not far behind.

"AND THAT GOES FOR YOU TOO, POSTBOX!"
"I AM DEEP UNDERCOVER FOR NEIGHBOURHOOD WATCH! DON'T GIVE THE GAME AWAY!" came a shout from inside the cardboard postbox.

Ben leaped over the fence into the playground. The postbox tumbled after him.

BOOF!

In a desperate bid to escape the postbox's clutches, Ben swung on the swing, slid down a slide and clambered up a climbing frame. Fortunately for Ben, Mr Parker couldn't see too well out of the slot. The postbox stumbled around in the dark before charging SLAP BANG into the climbing frame.

CLONK!

It fell to the ground.

There Mr Parker rolled around on his back like an upturned beetle, his legs waggling in the air.

"HELP ME, YOU FOOL! HELP!" came the cry from inside. "THIS IS A TOP-SECRET MISSION!"

"Give me a chance, you big red nincompoop!"

With difficulty, the park keeper helped the postbox to its feet. Ben chuckled to himself before making his escape through a hedge.

RUSTLE!

Ben now looked a lot like a hedge. He had twigs and leaves stuck to him. But he kept running.

His legs were racing. His heart was racing. His mind was racing. For all his eccentricities, Mr Parker had been right. The theft of Tutankhamun's mask did have all the hallmarks of **THE BLACK CAT.**

A daring robbery from a heavily guarded building.

A heist in the dead of night.

A figure dressed from head to toe in black.

A theft of something super famous and absolutely priceless.

A clue left behind in SCRABBLE letters.

Plus, and perhaps most importantly, this seemed like a theft done purely for the adventure.

The mask of Tutankhamun was not something that you would ever be able to sell. Who would buy something so famous that everyone in the world knew was stolen? You wouldn't be able to put it on display or ever sell it on. If you did, you would be arrested and thrown into prison. Forever!

Granny had told Ben that she only stole precious jewels for the thrill of it. She never sold a thing. But Granny had been gone a year, and Ben really had been fixing the toilet last night. If he'd stolen the mask of Tutankhamun, he would have remembered it!

Even so, this didn't put him in the clear. Mr Parker was convinced Ben was behind it. The boy was terrified that if he didn't find out who the real culprit was he would end up getting all the blame! Maybe Mr Parker would finally get his wish of seeing Ben behind bars!

Just when he thought things couldn't get any worse, Ben saw lights and heard music coming from his house. That meant only one thing. His mum and dad must be rehearsing another **ballroom-dancing** routine…

THE HORROR! THE HORROR!

Looking back, Ben couldn't see anyone following him, but to throw Mr Parker off the scent he sneaked down the alleyway and climbed over the wall. Then he made his way across his neighbours' back gardens, leaping over fences until he reached his. Outside, it was now pitch-black, but, inside, the house was illuminated by a disco ball and flashing coloured lights. The theme music from his parents' favourite TV show, **STRICTLY STARS DANCING**, was playing so loudly the house was shaking.

TA-DA-DA!

Ben pressed his face up against the glass sliding door. He peered into the living room. Mum and Dad were sporting matching ballroom outfits. Mum was in a sequined purple satin floor-length ball gown. Dad was in a matching sequined purple satin tight-fitting shirt and trousers with a cummerbund. They might have been dressed like professional dancers, but the truth was that the Herberts were anything but. All they were good at was hurling each other around the living room.

CRASH!

The armchair was bashed over on to its side.

BANG!

The coffee table was overturned.

WALLOP!

The floor lamp ended up upside down.

As Ben looked on in TERROR, his parents began a dance move that seemed destined for DISASTER!

Mum hoisted Dad into the air by his ankles. Then she began spinning him round the living room.

The problem was she was spinning him way too fast!

WHIRR!

Dad was nothing but a *BLUR!*

And it looked as if Mum, with her impossibly long false nails, might lose her grip at any moment.

Ben banged on the glass door and shouted, **"STOP!"**

"AAAHHH!" shrieked Mum. She was so startled to see a talking hedge outside in the dark that she accidentally let go of Dad!

SLIP!

"AAAAARRRGH!"

screamed Dad as he flew

through the air.

WHOOSH!

#

5

Ben looked on, helpless, from the other side of the glass as his father spun across the living room like a giant purple Frisbee.

WHIZZ!

He landed upside down on the sofa.

BOOMPH!

The force of the impact caused the sofa to topple over, taking him with it.

DUMT!

Just then the **STRICTLY STARS DANCING** theme tune ended with a huge TA-DA!

Mum unlocked the door to the garden, and Ben slid it open.

"Ooh, Ben! I didn't see you there! Why are you dressed like a hedge?"

"All the cool kids are doing it!"

"And what were you doing out there in the darkness?"

"Erm, just enjoying watching you dance," he lied. "Is Dad all right?"

"Oh no! I lost a nail!" said Mum, scouring the carpet. "Help me look for it!"

Ben spotted the long, fake, sparkly purple nail by the fireplace.

"Here it is!"

"Good boy!" she said, taking the nail and sticking it back into place. "And did you pick up **Ballroom Monthly?** My Flavio is on the cover!"

"Yes, Mum! I've got it right here!" he said as she snatched it out of his hand and began staring wistfully at the picture on the cover.

"Ooh, my little Flavi-pooh!" she cooed.

"Is Dad okay?"

"Oh! He's fine! This is the tenth time today! He

needs to learn to stop letting go of my hands with his ankles."

"EURGH!" came a moan from behind the sofa. Ben rushed over to him.

"Dad? Are you all right?"

"Me knee!" he whimpered, clearly in pain.

"That knee has caused him no end of trouble ever since he went down on it to propose to me. I had to help him up then!" said Mum.

"The sofa fell on me knee! Someone help me up! Please!" pleaded Dad.

Together Mum and Ben hoisted him to his feet.

"OOH!" screamed Dad as his leg straightened.

"What now, Pete?" asked Mum.

"Me knee's finally gone, Linda! I need to sit down!"

As all the things to sit on were in disarray, Mum guided him over to the coffee table. Dad went to sit down, only for one of the legs to poke him on the bottom.

"YOW!" he shrieked. "ME BOTTOM!"

The coffee table was upside down.

Ben used all his strength to right an armchair before lowering his father into it.

"OOF!" Dad exclaimed.

"Oh why, oh why, oh why did I marry you and your dodgy knee? I should have married Flavio Flavioli when I had the chance!" said Mum.

Flavio Flavioli was the most popular of the professional dancers on **STRICTLY STARS DANCING.** He was Mum's number-one pin-up. She was obsessed with the Italian ballroom champion, as were most women in Britain and plenty of men too. Mum had an impressive collection of Flavio Flavioli memorabilia, probably the largest in the world.

Apart from the photographs, posters and paintings of the dancer that adorned the walls (any pictures of Ben had been taken down to make room for them), Mum also had:

 a signed copy of Flavio's autobiography, *The Greatest Dancer the World Has Ever Known* (sadly signed "To Colin")...

a framed sock Flavio wore for the very first episode of **STRICTLY STARS DANCING** (unwashed)…

a Flavio Flavioli posable action figure (slightly chewed)…

a bottle of Flavio's very own perfume, **Whiff for Men**…

a jar of Flavio's earwax…

an official **STRICTLY STARS DANCING** toilet seat with a picture of Flavio on it…

a programme from Flavio's one-man touring dance extravaganza, *Me! Me! Me!*…

one of Flavio Flavioli's underarm hairs that an overeager fan had yanked out…

a pizza crust with his teeth marks in that he'd left on a plate in a restaurant seven years ago…

and one of Flavio's toenail clippings found in a hotel bath during last year's **STRICTLY** live tour.

"You never had any chance with Flavio!" exclaimed Dad.

Ben nodded.

"You met him once at Ben's dance competition! And that was only to give him mouth-to-mouth resuscitation when he was knocked out by a flying tap shoe!"

"I could tell Flavio liked me!"

"He was unconscious!"

"Knocked out by beauty!"

Hearing his mother going on and on about Flavio bored Ben stiff, so he quickly changed the subject. "Did you hear about the theft of Tutankhamun's mask?"

"Of course we did!" said Dad. "It's all over the TV!"

"Wall-to-wall news it is!" added Mum. "You can't get away from it! Why don't they just buy this King Tut fella a nice new mask and be done with it!"

"Who do you think stole it?" asked Ben.

Dad thought for a moment before replying, "A thief?"

"I know it's a thief, Dad! But who?"

"All I know is that it's someone who has five letters missing from their SCRABBLE set! No triple-word score for them! Now be a good boy and roll up my trouser leg, will you, Ben?"

It wasn't easy as the purple satin trousers were so

tight that it was as if they'd been sprayed on to Dad's legs. But, like rolling out the last bit of toothpaste from the tube, Ben finally squeezed Dad's leg out.

"OWEEE!" yelped Dad in pain when the trouser leg rolled over his big, squishy tomato of a knee.

"Ooh, you poor thing! That's nasty," said Mum.

"I won't be able to dance next week at the Royal Albert Hall!" Dad wailed, before descending into uncontrollable sobbing. "WAH! WAH! WAH!"

"What's all this about the Royal Albert Hall?" asked Ben. It was one of the most famous buildings in London, often called "the nation's village hall", as it was home to shows by the world's biggest superstars. It was not somewhere he would ever expect to see his parents perform.

"We wanted to surprise you!" said Mum. "We know how much you love **ballroom dancing**…"

Ben played along as best he could. "Oh yes. I love it. Nearly as much as I love plumbing."

"Plumbing's a pipe dream, boy," said Dad. "You need something sensible to fall back on."

"Like **ballroom dancing!**" added Mum. "Well, for your Christmas present this year we bought you a front-row seat to watch me and your father take part in a **ballroom-dancing** championship! At the Royal Albert Hall! In front of *the Queen!*"

Ben was in shock. How on earth did his mum and dad qualify for a **ballroom-dancing** championship? The kindest thing you could say about their dancing was that it was "enthusiastic".

"I don't know why you look so shocked, Benjamin!" said Mum.

She always called him Benjamin when he was in her bad books.

"Well, it's just, you know..." he spluttered.

"No! I don't know!"

Dad looked at his wife. "Well, Linda, you did lie a teeny-weeny bit on the application form."

"I might have written that we won some **ballroom-dancing** trophies that we haven't."

"You've never won one!" replied Ben.

"Not as yet, no."

"And you told me it was wrong to lie!"

"Yes, well, it's wrong if children lie, but it's okay for grown-ups."

Dad jumped in. "Your mother said that we were a very famous dance duo on the Outer Hebrides."

"The Outer Hebrides?" spluttered Ben. "You've never even been to Scotland, let alone the Outer Hebrides!"

"She said we were dance professionals in the Outer Hebrides' **STRICTLY STARS DANCING!**"

"Do they even have one?" asked Ben.

"No!" replied Mum. "But that's the beauty of the scheme! They can't check!"

Dad smiled and nodded. Ben sighed. His parents were both BONKERS!

"Well, I'm not going to miss my big moment in front of *Her Majesty the Queen!*" said Mum.

"Well, I am sorry, Linda, but you are going to have to!" snapped Dad. "My knee is not up to it."

Mum's eyes glowed with tears.

"Sorry, Mum," said Ben, holding her hand. "I guess

it's too late to find another dance partner for the big night."

"Hmmm. Maybe it's not TOO late," she replied, fixing her gaze on Ben. The boy turned to his father. Dad had fixed his gaze on him too.

"You don't mean…" spluttered Ben, "ME?"

Mum and Dad nodded.

"NOOOOOOOOOOOOOOOOOOOOOOOOOOO OOOOOOOOOOOOOOOOOOOOOOOOOOOO OOO!" he cried.

6

"There is no way I am ever, ever, ever dancing again!" shouted Ben.

"Not even with your own mother?" pleaded Mum.

"Especially not with my own mother! In case it wasn't weird enough, that just makes it a billion times weirder!"

"I'll tell you what is weirderest,* Benjamin. A boy your age spending all night with his hands down a U-bend!"

"There was a blockage!"

"Don't use rude words like that in front of your mother!" chided Dad.

"It's not rude! Listen! There is absolutely no way

---

* See your **Walliamsictionary** *for confirmation that this is a real made-up word.*

I am ever **ballroom dancing** with you in front of *the Queen!*"

Mum turned her head and looked towards the window.

"Are you all right, Mum?"

"I just have something in my eye, that's all," she replied, followed by fake sobbing. "BOO! HOO! HOO!"

Ben looked at his father, who seemed even more clueless as to what to do than he did.

"Goodnight!" chirped Ben, before dashing through the door and racing upstairs to his bedroom.

He flicked on the light.

CLICK!

Ben's bedroom was full of little reminders of Granny.

There were a couple of framed photographs of her: one of Ben and Granny together, and another black-and-white photograph of Granny looking glamorous in her younger days. It served as a wonderful reminder that old people weren't always old. They have had a lifetime of adventure before you were even born.

There were some tins of Granny's cabbage soup on the shelf. Ben had absolutely no desire to eat the soup – he didn't like the bitter taste. However, looking at them always made him smile. Cabbage soup was what he'd always eaten when he'd stayed over at Granny's house.

Under his bed, Ben had the most precious of her possessions: the Silver Jubilee biscuit tin in which she'd kept her jewels hidden. Ben had rescued it from the charity shop in exchange for unblocking their toilet. Finding that tin was how the adventure had begun. Ben thought that one day, if he were lucky enough to be a grandpa, he would leave some jewels in there for his grandchild to find and take them on a whole new adventure.

When Ben passed by his bedroom window, something caught his eye. He peered out. Something was moving on one of the rooftops opposite. Ben ducked and shuffled back over to the door on his knees to turn out the light.

CLICK!

Now he couldn't be seen from the outside. He grabbed a piece of metal pipe on the end of which he'd stuck the lens of a magnifying glass to make a telescope. Keeping low, he put his eye to it and scanned the rooftops.

"The **black cat!**" hissed Ben.

It was the same **black cat** the boy had seen in the graveyard. He could tell by the way it moved – like a panther. It slunk across the snow-dusted rooftops. This cat was certainly not a scaredy-cat, as it leaped from roof to roof. Ben trained the telescope on to its face. It turned to look at him, seemed to smile and then it made another daring leap

and disappeared from view.

7

THE COOLEST KID IN THE WORLD

"Who would do such a thing?" said Dad from the breakfast table the next morning as he read his newspaper. He was wearing his security-guard uniform, but had his trouser leg rolled up and a bag of frozen peas resting on his sore knee. Mum was sitting next to him, reading her **Ballroom Monthly.**

"Do what, Dad?" asked Ben as he took his seat next to him and spread some jam on his toast.

"Look, son."

The story was so DRAMATIC it took up the entire FRONT PAGE!

The International News

WORLD CUP
STOLEN!

The FIFA World Cup trophy was stolen last night in a daring heist. The priceless and world-famous gold trophy depicts two figures holding up the globe. It was on display at Wembley Stadium as it tours different nations ahead of the next tournament. The trophy was stolen in the dead of night by a figure dressed head to toe in black. Just as with the dramatic theft of the death mask of the Ancient Egyptian pharaoh Tutankhamun, the thief left behind a clue to their identity. This time, on the plinth where the World Cup had been on display was a word spelled out in Scrabble letters: PURR. The police are convinced this is the same thief who stole the Ancient Egyptian death mask. However, so far, they have no leads whatsoever. They are asking anyone who knows anything about the crime to come forward immediately.

Ben gulped.

He'd been tucked up in BED the whole night.

He didn't even *like* FOOTBALL.

He had ZERO interest in the **WORLD CUP**.

BUT Mr Parker was sure to pin the BLAME on Ben.

The boy had to do some detective work. Otherwise, he would find himself thrown into prison for a crime he hadn't committed!

"The **WORLD CUP!** It's the most beautiful thing in the world!" sobbed Dad, mopping his eyes with his sleeve.

"No," corrected Mum, not looking up from her **Ballroom Monthly.** "The most beautiful thing in the world is Flavio's face!"

"Not him again," muttered Dad.

"And – oh, my word! – it says here that he is going to be hosting the ballroom competition at the Albert Hall! Ben! Please! I have to do it! And I can't enter alone! Please, please, please be my dance partner!"

Mum got down on her knees and begged.

Ben looked to his dad for help, but the man hid behind his newspaper.

"I have thought long and hard about this," began Ben.

"YES?" said Mum expectantly.

"And it's still a big fat no!"

Mum wailed, "But why, Ben, why?"

There were a BILLION reasons, and there wasn't enough time to list them all now. Instead, Ben stuffed a whole piece of toast in his mouth.

"Sorry, I have to dash right now," he mumbled, barely making any sense because he had so much food in his mouth.

"What are you saying? Where are you going?" demanded Mum.

"OUT!" exclaimed Ben, spraying toast crumbs everywhere.

SPLIT! SPLUT! SPLOT!

He stood up from the table.

"Ben! Tell me! Where are you off to?" demanded Mum.

The boy stuffed another piece of toast into his already full mouth. Now he could say anything at all and there'd be no chance of anyone understanding it, so he made up some silly gobbledygook.

"Mnuma noodflumph fibble-fobble shimalong groobyponk!"

Mum and Dad looked at their son in utter confusion.

"You what what?" asked Dad.

"Well, just don't be late for tea!" added Mum.

Ben dashed out of the kitchen door and into the garage. There, a rather special vehicle was waiting for him.

It was Granny's old mobility scooter. She'd left it to Ben in her will. He hadn't been given permission to ride it yet on account of only being twelve, but Ben knew this was an EMERGENCY. If he asked his parents, they would just say no, so Ben's logic was that it was best not to ask them. SIMPLE!

In the past year, the boy had added some bits and pieces to make it **SUPERFLY!**

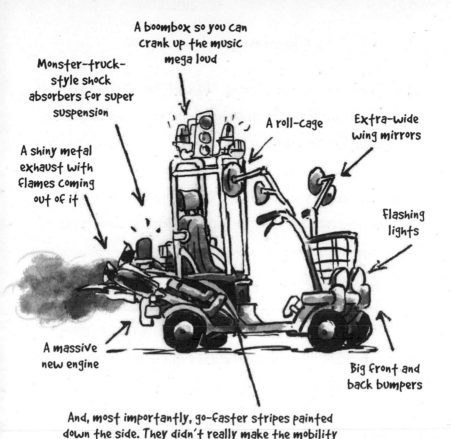

A boombox so you can crank up the music mega loud

Monster-truck-style shock absorbers for super suspension

A roll-cage

Extra-wide wing mirrors

A shiny metal exhaust with flames coming out of it

Flashing lights

A massive new engine

Big front and back bumpers

And, most importantly, go-faster stripes painted down the side. They didn't really make the mobility scooter go any faster, but they looked COOL!

The only problem was that Granny had named her mobility scooter **Millicent.** The name didn't quite suit this beast of a machine now, but Ben felt it was wrong to change it. So he leaped on to it, and shouted, "Come on, **Millicent!** Let's burn some rubber!"

Slowly, the mobility scooter rolled out of the

garage. Despite all the modifications, it didn't go all that much faster than before! It might be quicker to walk, but Ben thought he'd be the envy of all the kids in town because he was riding his very own SUPER SCOOTER!

He cranked up the hip-hop music and whirred through the streets.

WHIRR!

Ben got some funny looks from passers-by. No matter. He felt like the coolest kid in the world.

What's more, it brought back happy memories of riding shotgun with Granny on the most exciting night of his life. His eyes glistened. Whether it was at the memory of it or because of the wind, he wasn't sure.

Ben's destination was the local library. There, he could find books about the British Museum and Wembley Stadium. If he could study those buildings like he had the Tower of London, he might be able to work out how the thief had broken in. There could be a clue to their identity.

All the while, as Ben trundled along the pavement, he checked the wing mirrors to see if anyone was following. He paid particularly close attention to postboxes in case one moved.

None did.

Soon Ben had reached the library. He performed a sharp turn and a skid.

SCREECH!

Millicent shuddered to a halt SLAP BANG outside the library door. That was one of the great things about driving a mobility scooter: you could park it anywhere!

Ben pushed open the double doors to the library and marched in.

He meant business!

8

LOW-SPEED CHASE

"Excuse me?" said Ben to the librarian standing behind the counter.

"Shush!" shushed the woman, pointing to a sign that read: **THIS IS A LIBRARY. FOR GOODNESS' SAKE, BE QUIET!**

The stern old lady wore half-moon spectacles, which perched on her large nose. She stared through them at the boy.

"Excuse me!" whispered Ben. "Where would I find picture books of famous buildings like the British Museum and Wembley Stadium, please?"

"Architecture section. You will find it in non-fiction," she replied, pointing.

"Thank you," said Ben, and he turned to go.

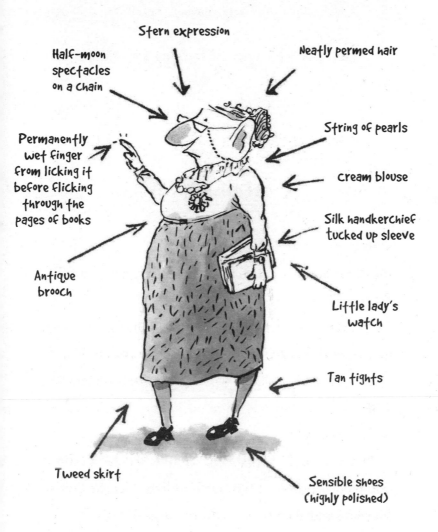

Stern expression

Neatly permed hair

Half-moon spectacles on a chain

String of pearls

Permanently wet finger from licking it before flicking through the pages of books

cream blouse

Silk handkerchief tucked up sleeve

Antique brooch

Little lady's watch

Tan tights

Tweed skirt

Sensible shoes (highly polished)

Suddenly a thought flashed across the librarian's face. She looked mightily suspicious. Both buildings Ben had named had been in the news.

"May I ask why you are looking for said books?" she hissed.

"You may ask, yes, but I'm not going to tell you!" replied Ben.

The librarian's already sour face soured some more. "I demand to know the answer!"

Ben leaned in and whispered so nobody else could hear him. "I'm on a top-secret mission and all information is on a need-to-know basis. And I'm sorry, but you don't need to know!"

The lady's red eyes narrowed. Ben was sure she reminded him of someone. He just couldn't place who. There wasn't time to ponder it any further as he had to get to work.

"Goodbye!" he chirped, skipping off.

Ben's eyes scanned the spines until he found the books he was looking for. There was one called **Museums of London** and another, **STADIUMS OF THE WORLD,** which he took off the shelves. He sat on the floor and flicked through the pages to find plans of both buildings. It made for intriguing reading.

The British Museum was a beautiful old building with Greek-style columns at the front. The only weakness on the outside that Ben could spot were the windows to the round Reading Room, the huge domed library of the museum. Perhaps one could be forced open at night without detection, as they were so high up. However, getting up the outside and getting down the inside both seemed impossible, especially with the solid gold mask of Tutankhamun, which must weigh a tonne.

There was a footnote about some tunnels that had been built deep underground in London during World War Two to escape from the Nazi bombing. The tunnels connected some important buildings like the British Museum, the Ministry of Defence, the Houses of Parliament, 10 Downing Street (the home of the prime minister) and Buckingham Palace (the home of the royal family). However, these were all thought to have been impassable for decades.

Next, Ben moved on to study Wembley Stadium. The only way in at night that he could spot was flying overhead and landing right on the football pitch! But how could anyone do that undetected? Planes and helicopters were super noisy. It just didn't make sense. Although, there *was* a high-tech sprinkler system underneath the pitch. Perhaps an expert plumber could find a way in from underground somehow.

As he was brooding over all this, Ben noticed a pair of **red eyes** spying on him through the bookshelf. Red eyes framed by half-moon spectacles. The moment he fixed his gaze on the nosy librarian, she turned away sharply, and pretended to be restacking the shelf.

Ben thought it best to take the books out of the library. That way he could study them in peace. He rushed to the counter, hoping a different librarian would help him, but no – the elderly lady broke into a run and intercepted him.

"Just these two, is it?" she hissed.

"Yes. Thank you!"

The librarian studied the books for a moment, and then looked at the boy with deep suspicion. "Just wait here a moment, please. I need to telephone the chief librarian."

Now it was Ben's turn to be suspicious. This had never happened when he'd taken out one of the library's plumbing books before.

"Why?" he asked.

"I need to check that the books haven't been reserved by anyone else."

With that, she snatched the books from his grip, and put them just out of his reach on the counter. Next, she marched over to the telephone. It was old-fashioned like her, and she kept her beady eyes on Ben as she dialled the number.

The librarian covered her mouth so Ben couldn't

hear, which he thought was odd.

While she was on the telephone, he spotted a lady even older and sterner than this one march past the counter. The name badge pinned to her chest read:

MRS MOST: CHIEF LIBRARIAN

The librarian with the half-moon spectacles couldn't be speaking to the chief librarian! It was all a lie!

The librarian hadn't seen her boss. After she'd put the telephone down, she hissed, "The chief librarian just asked you to wait here for a moment."

"That's strange," remarked Ben.

"What's strange?"

"I just saw the chief librarian walk past you."

Now the librarian's face **soured** so much Ben thought it might turn inside out. He looked at her name badge. It read:

MISS PARKER: LIBRARIAN

She looked exactly like Mr Parker! Well, not exactly, but there was a very strong resemblance. The nosy nose especially. Could she be the nosy neighbour's sister?

"Please hand over your library card so I can check your details on our file," said Miss Parker.

"No!" snapped Ben. He leaped up and grabbed hold of the books. Then he made a run for it towards the double doors.

"I HAVEN'T STAMPED THOSE BOOKS YET!" shouted Miss Parker. Her voice echoed throughout the library.

"Shush!" said Ben, pointing towards the sign that read: **THIS IS A LIBRARY. FOR GOODNESS' SAKE, BE QUIET!**

He charged out of the doors with the books stuffed under his arms. Looking behind, he could see that Miss Parker was chasing after him.

Ben flung the books into **Millicent's** basket, and then took off!

WHIRR!

Checking behind him, he spotted Miss Parker leaping on her mobility scooter in pursuit.

WHIRR!

This was a

LOW-SPEED CHASE!

9

GIANT FRUIT LOLLY

"Come on, **Millicent!** Come on, old girl! You can do it!" cried Ben as he tapped the mobility scooter in the hope she would go faster.

WHIRR!

Ben and Miss Parker were now racing along the pavement. Shoppers on the high street were leaping out of the way!

"WATCH OUT!"

"HELP!"

"STOP THAT BOY!"

All the while, Miss Parker was gaining on him. She was slapping her mobility scooter's behind with a heavy book.

THUMP! THUMP! THUMP!

"Come on, Virginia!" she cried, and Virginia put a spurt on!

WHIRRR!

Do all old folks give their mobility scooters names as if they're horses? thought Ben. There wasn't time to ponder it further because Miss Parker was now speeding alongside him.

"YOU ARE IN BIG TROUBLE, YOU WORM!" she shouted.

"I will bring the books back first thing tomorrow! I promise!" he replied.

While turning to shout at Miss Parker, he'd not seen what was ahead: a grocer's shop with all its fruit and vegetables on display outside. Ben ploughed straight into it.

SHUNT!

SPLURGE!

He was totally **GUNGED!**

The boy was covered from head to toe in:

Tomatoes

Blackberries

Plums

Gooseberries

Grapes

Watermelon

Bananas

Raspberries

Peaches

Mangos

BEFORE

AFTER

He looked like a giant fruit lolly!

"OI!" shouted the greengrocer. "COME BACK HERE!"

"I'm sorry!" Ben called out. "I can't stop right now!"

CLUNK! CLONK! CLINK!

Ben looked down and saw that Miss Parker was bashing her mobility scooter into his.

"What are you doing?" demanded Ben.

"Finish her off, Virginia!" Miss Parker called out, bashing the back of her scooter with a book again.

THUMP!

She yanked the handlebars sharply to the left, forcing Ben down an alleyway.

"HA! HA!" laughed Miss Parker.

"What's so funny?"

"You are trapped!"

"No! I am not!"

Ben knew there was a car park up ahead. He could escape through that!

However, as soon as he sped into it, he saw Mr Parker waiting for him on his tricycle!

Ben skidded to a halt.

S C R E E C H !

He looked left. He looked right. Surrounding him was an army of oldies. A dozen or more. All on various modes of transport.

Mobility scooter

Walker

Electric
wheelchair

Motorised tricycle

Go-cart

Rollator (a walking frame on wheels)

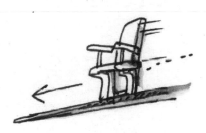

Specially adapted stairlift
chair that goes sideways
instead of up and down

Bath on wheels

Space hopper

Supermarket trolley

Motorised armchair

Donkey

The oldies formed a circle round Ben.

The boy was trapped!

10

"Miaow! Or should I say PURR!" called out Mr Parker from his tricycle.

"I don't know what you are talking about," protested Ben.

"Oh yes you do, Benjamin Herbert!"

"Ben is fine," replied the boy. "By the way, hello, everybody! Lovely day for it!" he called out to the group. Ben liked old folk and they liked him. But this lot assembled in the car park scowled back at him. They must have been told he was the wickedest boy on Earth.

"I see you've met my sister, Miss Parker," continued Mr Parker, indicating the lady blocking

Ben's escape from behind.

"Yep!" replied Ben. "We've really hit it off!"

"She telephoned me from the library."

"I guessed that."

Mr Parker looked peeved that the boy was one step ahead of him.

"She told me all about the books you were taking out!"

"I guessed that too!"

"Books that link you directly to the crimes."

"Can I just say something?"

"Could you please stop interrupting me?"

"Yep!"

"Thank you."

"No problem."

"BE QUIET!"

"Got it!" replied Ben, and he mimed zipping up his mouth.

Some of the oldies chuckled.

"HA! HA!"

This made Mr Parker furious. "Silence! I've gathered

every single member of the local **Neighbourhood Watch** group to apprehend you. Benjamin Hilary Herbert, with the powers I have invested in myself, I hereby conduct a citizen's arrest on you!"

"Me?" exclaimed Ben, still sitting on Granny's mobility scooter. "THIS IS NUTS!"

"Because you were the accomplice to a jewel thief! You are still using her getaway vehicle! And I firmly believe you are behind these dastardly crimes! How else could you explain your choice of books, which link you directly to them?"

"Which," interjected Miss Parker, "the boy did not have stamped out of the library!"

"TUT! TUT! TUT!" went the oldies. It was clear they regarded this as a DEADLY SERIOUS CRIME.

Ben hung his fruit-gunged head in shame.

"What have you got to say for yourself, boy?" demanded Mr Parker.

"Please listen. If I'd stolen Tutankhamun's mask and the **WORLD CUP,** I would hardly take these books out of the library *after* the thefts, now, would I? I would take them out before!"

This silenced Mr Parker for a moment.

"True!"

"He has a point!"

"What did he say?" muttered the oldies.

"It could be a DOUBLE BLUFF!" said Mr Parker from his motorised tricycle.

"Ooh yes."

"A double bluff!"

"A double what, dear?"

"BLUFF!"

"GUFF?"

"NO: BLUFF!"

"Ooh, right!" muttered the oldies again.

"There is no double bluff!" replied Ben.

"A triple bluff, then!" snarled Miss Parker.

"How would that work?" asked her brother.

"I don't know, but it sounds good!"

"Listen!" said Ben. "There is no double bluff or triple bluff or quadruple bluff or any other bluff. I got out these books because I'm trying to find out who committed the crime!"

"A likely story!"

"What rot!"

"Claptrap!"

"Twaddle, twuddle and twiddle!"

"Lock him up and throw away the key!" cried the oldies.

"Pipe down, please!" ordered Mr Parker, and they fell silent. "Now, boy, I don't want any fuss. If you will kindly accompany me to the nearest police station…"

The fuzz! thought Ben. *What if they do some digging about that night at the Tower of London?*

He could end up in a huge dollop of TROUBLE!

"Yes, of course," he lied, before yanking hard on the throttle.

WHIRR!

Millicent the mobility scooter sped off.

VROOM!

"AFTER HIM!" shouted Mr Parker.

Ben raced around the car park, but one by one the

Neighbourhood Watch group shut off all his escape routes.

"WE HAVE YOU SURROUNDED!" cried Miss Parker. "GIVE YOURSELF UP!"

Ben yanked on the throttle again and did a wheelie.

VROOM!

Millicent's front wheels lifted off the ground and mounted a super-low Italian sports car that had been left in the car park.

CRUNK! went the mobility scooter's wheels as it ran over the roof of the car.

CRUNK! And another.

CRUNK! And another!

Ben was riding **Millicent** up and down the bonnets and boots of all the cars in the car park.

"GET HIM!" shouted Mr Parker. He yanked up the front wheel of his tricycle to chase the boy.

However, Mr Parker picked the wrong car to ride over, as there was a driver inside! It was Raj in his battered old red Reliant Robin three-wheeler with **RAJ RACER** emblazoned on the side.

"Go, Ben, go!" called out Raj as he drove off with Mr Parker on his roof.

"Raj! You're the best! Thanks a billion!"

"STOP!" shouted Mr Parker. He slammed on his brakes…

SQUEAK!

…as he was being driven out

of the car park on top of the *RAJ RACER!*

BRUMM!

The oldies all looked on in disbelief.

"DON'T JUST SIT THERE! HELP ME!" cried Mr Parker.

All the **Neighbourhood Watch** group chased after their leader as he was driven down the high street on the roof of Raj's Reliant Robin while Ben made his escape!

He sped all the way home and hid the mobility scooter back in the garage.

"Thanks a million, **Millicent.** You did me and Granny proud today!" he said as he plugged her in for a recharge. "Get some of this down you!"

Ben said hello to his mum, who was busy cutting out pictures from **Ballroom Monthly** and sticking them into her already full-to-bursting Flavio Flavioli scrapbook. His dad was out at work at the supermarket, guarding tins of baked beans with his life.

Ben went straight to his bedroom. Once safely inside, he allowed himself a giant sigh of relief. "HURR!" That had been close…

But no sooner had he sat on his bed than there was a sound.

DING! DONG!

It was the doorbell. Ben gulped. He let his mother answer it. Then he peeked out of his bedroom window to see who it was.

Parked up outside his house was a POLICE CAR!

Instantly, Ben felt as if he were going to explode in

PANIC!

He tiptoed over to his bedroom door and opened it the tiniest sliver so he could listen.

"Mrs Herbert?" came a familiar voice from downstairs.

"Yes!" replied Mum anxiously.

"I am PC Fudge. May I come in?

It's about your boy..."

11

Ben had met the policeman before. Police Constable Fudge had stopped Granny and Ben that night they'd ridden **Millicent** on a motorway when they went to London to steal the *Crown Jewels.* The pair had bamboozled him with some silly excuse as to why they were wearing wetsuits and had miles of clingfilm. They'd told him they were going to an underwater meeting of the **CLINGFILM APPRECIATION SOCIETY!** Miraculously, Fudge had believed them!

The kindly PC ended up giving the unlikely pair of international jewel thieves a lift in his police car all the way to the Tower of London. Then, when they'd finally arrived home and Mr Parker accused them of stealing the *Crown Jewels*, Fudge ended up being their alibi. When Fudge spoke up in their defence, Granny and Ben were let off the hook. An extraordinary night of policing from PC Fudge!

Fudge was a large man with a tiny moustache, which only served to make his big, round face look even bigger and rounder. He was the model of modern policing:

Cap at a jaunty angle

Tiny moustache

Coffee stains

Police badge on upside down

Too-tight shirt

Doughnut dust

Walkie-talkie tuned into local country-music station: Cowboy FM

Biscuit crumbs

Too-tight trousers

Pie flakes

As Mum led PC Fudge into the living room, Ben tiptoed down the stairs so he could hear what was being said.

"One of our local **Neighbourhood Watch** group leaders has just presented himself at the police station to report your son."

"Who?" demanded Mum.

"I can't say."

"Was it Mr Parker?"

"Yes."

"Reporting Ben? Whatever for?"

"The list of crimes is long, madam."

"I can't believe it! He's always such a good boy!"

"That's what they all say!"

"Whatever has he done?"

"Taking not one but two books out of the library without having them stamped."

"Can you be thrown in prison for that?"

"If you never, ever, ever return them, then yes, possibly."

"Oh no."

"Being rude to a group of pensioners."

"Really? My Ben? He's normally so good with old folk, like my husband."

"Driving over parked cars on a mobility scooter."

"It gets worse! I am so sorry. This is awful! You know who I blame?"

"His mother?" asked PC Fudge.

"No! That's me!"

"Oh yes! So it is."

From his hiding place, Ben stifled a chuckle.

"His grandmother!" continued Mum.

"Is that so?"

"Oh yes! They became very close. And, just before she died, Granny put all sorts of silly ideas in that boy's head."

"Did she now?"

From the other side of the door, Ben gulped.

G U L P!

"Yes! Left him that mobility scooter in her will, can you believe? He was told he couldn't ride it until he was a grown-up! Don't you worry, PC Fudge! I will confiscate his keys at once!"

"If you would, please!"

"I am absolutely shocked! Would you like a cup of tea, PC Fudge? I just made a pot."

"Yes, please, madam. Have you got any biscuits?"

"Of course! I should have asked! How many would you like?"

"Oh! Just one…"

"Right."

"…packet."

"Jammy Dodgers okay?"

"My favourite!"

From outside the living-room door, Ben swallowed his fury. They were his Jammy Dodgers! His favourite biscuit in the universe! *Don't let Fudge scoff the lot!* There was a short silence when Mum disappeared off to the kitchen.

"Here you go," she said on returning.

"Ooh! Thank you," replied PC Fudge.

There followed the sounds of slurping and munching.

SLURP!

CRUNCH! MUNCH!

SLURP!

Then a burp.

"BURP! Pardon
me!"

"Pardoned! Is
there anything else
you need to tell me,
PC Fudge? I feel
that if there is, this
mother's heart will break!"

Mum was always very THEATRICAL!

"Yes, madam. And this is where it becomes more
serious."

"More serious than riding a mobility scooter over
parked cars?"

"I am afraid so."

"Please put me out of my misery! I beg of you!"

"Your son, Benjamin Herbert, has been accused of
stealing the mask of Tutankhamun..."

There was the sound of tea being sprayed across the living room.

SPLURT!

"Noooooo! I need another gulp of tea to get over the shock!" exclaimed Mum.

"And the **WORLD CUP!**"

SPLURT!

More tea was sprayed.

"Oh, did a little bit go on you, PC Fudge?" asked Mum.

"Just a tiny drop!"

Ben peered through the gap in the door. The policeman was being polite. He was covered from head to toe in tea.

"You think my Benjamin is behind these thefts?" Mum asked incredulously.

"The police have no leads, and an accusation has been made against your son, madam. We have to take it deadly seriously."

"BENJAMIN!" she shouted.

"Yes!" said Ben, trying to throw his voice so it

sounded as if he were still upstairs and not standing right outside the living-room door.

"COME DOWNSTAIRS AT ONCE!"

"I am just fixing that leaky tap!" he lied.

"The leaky tap can wait! COME DOWNSTAIRS THIS INSTANT!"

Ben then made the sound of his feet coming down the stairs.

STOMP! STOMP! STOMP!

He stomped quietly at first before becoming louder and louder, until he burst through the door, breathless.

"What on earth is it, Mum?" he spluttered.

"Well, well, well. We meet again, young man," said PC Fudge.

"You two have met before?" asked Mum.

All eyes turned to Ben.

12

GROUNDED!

"Benjamin!" began Mum. "I think you have some explaining to do!"

"About what?" asked Ben as he stood in the doorway to the living room. PC Fudge and his mother were both giving him disapproving looks!

"Boy, we've had some complaints from a member of the **Neighbourhood Watch,** Lower Toddle branch," began the policeman.

"Who?" asked Ben.

"I'm not at liberty to say."

"Mr Parker?"

"Yes. Oh! I shouldn't have said that. It might be Mr Parker; it might not."

"It *is* him, though."

"Yes," replied PC Fudge, before slapping his forehead in frustration.

THWACK!

"What's all this about stealing Tutankhamun's mask and the **WORLD CUP?** If you needed extra pocket money, then you just needed to ask!" said Mum.

"I didn't steal them!" protested Ben.

"Well, the **Neighbourhood Watch** man Mr Parker thinks you did!"

"That man's a menace! He's accused me of all sorts of ridiculous stuff!"

"Like what?" asked Mum.

"Stealing the *Crown Jewels* from the Tower of London!" interjected PC Fudge.

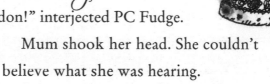

Mum shook her head. She couldn't believe what she was hearing.

"Did you steal the *Crown Jewels*, Benjamin?" she asked gravely.

"NO!" he replied. "Of course not!"

Ben was only half lying. He and Granny had tried

to steal them, but when they'd been discovered by the Queen they'd fled the scene empty-handed.

"That was the first time I came across your son, madam," said Fudge. "Just over a year ago, if my memory serves me well. It was very late at night and the boy was out with his grandmother."

"I knew it! The old goat was always up to no good! What were you doing out late at night with your granny, Benjamin?" Mum demanded.

"Well, er, um, we were just… you know," spluttered Ben.

"No! I don't know!"

"You were going to a meeting of the CLINGFILM APPRECIATION SOCIETY," said Fudge.

"Oh yes! Thank you for reminding me!" said Ben, trying to sound pleased but failing miserably.

"You don't appreciate clingfilm!" exclaimed Mum. "You have never appreciated clingfilm! You like to have your packed lunch wrapped in tinfoil!"

PC Fudge's little eyes narrowed and his moustache twitched. "Now I don't know what to believe!"

"I do appreciate clingfilm!" said Ben. "It's just your egg sandwiches pong a bit and the tinfoil keeps the stink in!"

"How dare you insult my egg sandwiches!"

"Perhaps we should have a talk down at the police station, Benjamin," said Fudge.

Mum threw herself at the policeman's knees. "Please don't arrest him, PC Fudge! I beg of you! I will die of shame!"

"Right now, we don't have enough evidence to arrest your son."

"Phew!" said Ben.

"But we will be investigating further."

"Of course. You have to. But right now, PC Fudge, what should I do with him?"

"Madam, don't let this boy out of your sight!" declared Fudge, pointing at Ben.

"Don't you worry about that, PC Fudge!" she replied. "Benjamin Herbert, you are well and truly…

GROUNDED!"

13

NUMBER-ONE SUSPECT

"M-U-M!" moaned Ben as soon as PC Fudge had left, taking a packet of custard creams "for the road".

"Don't you M-U-M me!" snapped Mum. "I'm not having the whole street see a police car parked outside our house again! The shame!"

"But it's not fair! You can't ground me. I've done nothing wrong."

"Taking books out of the library without getting them stamped. Being rude to a group of do-gooding pensioners! Driving Granny's mobility scooter over some cars!"

"Well, yes, apart from all that, of course, absolutely nothing!"

"Anyway, you can use all the time stuck at home—"

"Fixing the boiler?" asked Ben hopefully.

"No! No! No!" said Mum. "Something so much more important…!"

Ben knew she could only mean one thing. "**Ballroom dancing?**" asked Ben.

"How did you guess?" she exclaimed, performing a little **cha~cha~cha** across the living-room floor.

Ben was forming an idea. An idea that might just set him free. It was a disaster to be grounded when he was under so much suspicion, not just from the **Neighbourhood Watch** group, but also now the police. He needed to carry on with his detective work. That was the only way he could stop being the NUMBER-ONE SUSPECT.

If he agreed to take part in the dance competition, then he'd have to be allowed out.

No more being grounded!

There were just a couple of problems.

First, he would have to dance in front of the Queen! Ben's parents knew nothing about his and Granny's midnight meeting with her at the Tower of London. What if the Queen recognised him? She might very well give the game away. Then the boy would have some serious explaining to do.

Second, and more importantly, Ben couldn't dance! Not at all! Not one step!

But all this was better than being thrown in prison for a crime he hadn't committed! If Ben couldn't get out there and discover who the real thief was, then that was sure to happen.

Ben took a deep breath. He would have to play this next scene like an award-winning actor.

"M-u-m," began Ben.

"Yes, Benjamin?"

"I was just thinking about your offer to be your ballroom-dancing partner…"

"Oh yes?" asked Mum.

The boy had the prize fish hooked. Now he just had to reel her in.

"And I have decided…"

"Yes?"

"…that I'll do it!"

"YES!" exclaimed Mum, literally jumping for joy.

"If!"

"Oh!"

"If…"

"I didn't know there was an if."

"I'll do it only if I'm not grounded! If I'm grounded, then I won't be able to go to the Royal Albert Hall to dance with you, will I?"

It had a certain twisted logic to it.

"Mmm… I'll have to think long and hard about this," said Mum.

Then, after half a second, she said, "BENJAMIN! THE GROUNDING PERIOD IS NOW OVER!"

It was the shortest amount of time any child had ever been grounded! Less than a minute!

"YES!" cried Ben, before his face turned into a picture of **FEAR.** Now there was no getting out of it.

As for Mum, she was too busy waltzing around the living room in celebration to notice.

"A mother-and-son dancing duo! The public are going to love us! First the Royal Albert Hall, and then the world!"

"The what?" spluttered Ben.

"You are right! One step at a time! We only have until Sunday!"

"*Sunday?*"

"That's the night of the competition. Just under a week away! Now first I need to get going on our costumes!" Mum held up the sleeve of her dress to her son's face. "Purple is not your colour."

"Thank goodness for that!"

"You need something lighter. I know! PINK!"

"What the…?"

Before Ben could say a rude word, Dad arrived home from work at the supermarket.

"I saw a police car outside the house," he said, limping in. "What was it doing here?"

"Oh! Never mind about all that!" replied Mum, to Ben's astonishment. "The big news is that Ben is going to be my brand-new **ballroom-dancing** partner!"

"GOOD BOY!" cried Dad. "I knew that **ballroom dancing** was in your blood, son!"

"Yep," replied Ben. Before he could utter another word, Mum had taken him by the hands and spun him round the living room.

"COME ON, SON!" she cried, happier than she'd ever been before. **"LET'S DANCE!"**

PART TWO

DANCE
INTO
DANGER

14

TWO LEFT FEET

Ben was beginning to wish PC Fudge had thrown him in prison after all.

The next week was the worst of the boy's life.

First, Mum insisted on putting him in a series of home-made ~~ballroom-dancing~~ costumes.

They were all on a scale that started with embarrassing, continued to hideously embarrassing and went all the way to horrifically embarrassing.

Every outfit had a theme.

There was:

The Pineapple

Harlequinade

The Windmill

Jelly Baby

Godzilla vs Kong

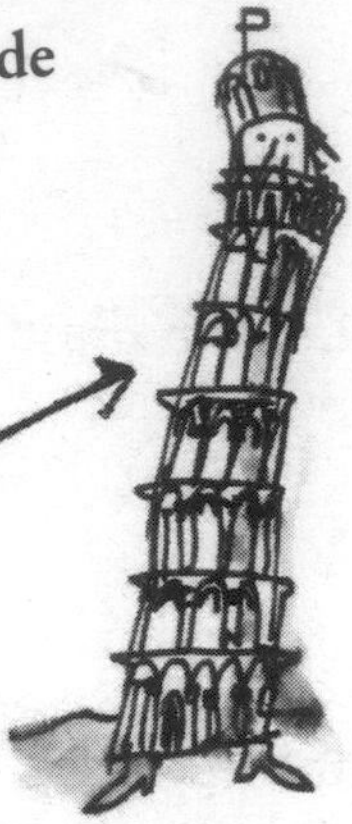

The Leaning Tower of Pisa

The Cactus

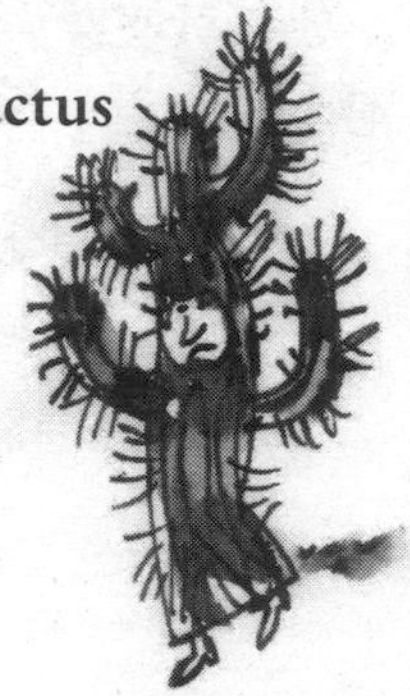

Cleopatra

The Prawn

Buck's Fizz

Hercules

Butterflies

Fairy Cake

The Dance of a Hundred Balloons

Nuts, Nuts, Hazelnuts!

The Rainbow

Liquid Gold

The Faun

The Mirror Ball

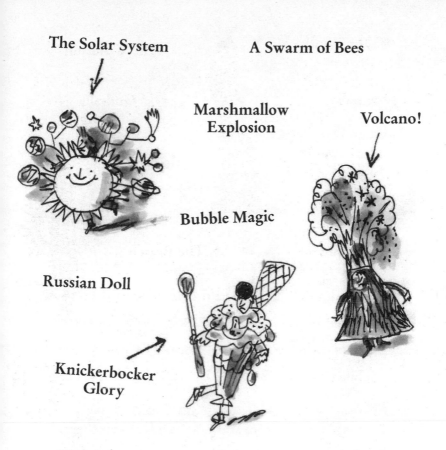

The Solar System

A Swarm of Bees

Marshmallow
Explosion

Volcano!

Bubble Magic

Russian Doll

Knickerbocker
Glory

Mum's least-worst creation was a costume simply called **iceberg.** This wasn't because it was put in the freezer before Ben put it on. No, it was an all-white all-in-one bodysuit with lots of lumps and bumps that were meant to resemble a huge block of ice.

When you put it on and moved around, the overall effect was that of a giant dancing slushy!

"This one could be worse," said Ben.

"You love it! Splendid!" cooed Mum. "And I am so pleased you chose that one as I have a brilliant idea for a routine for us. The story of the *Titanic*!"

"The ship that was sunk by an iceberg!" spluttered Ben.

"Yes! I am the ship, and you will be the iceberg!"

"A ship and an iceberg can't dance together!"

Mum was most displeased. "Let's have a bit of a better attitude, please! In the world of **ballroom dancing,** anything is possible!"

So she set out to prove this. All day, every day, Ben had to rehearse the dance routine with his mum. It was all set to the famous song from the film *Titanic*,

"My Heart Will Go On". He'd heard it so many times he wanted to cry every time the first note struck up.

Despite being only twelve and short for his age, the boy had to lift, hold and even spin his mum during the dramatic routine she had devised. This would have been easier for Dad, but that knee injury of his meant he would now be watching from the front row.

Mum's outfit was equally as bonkers as her son's. She was going to represent the RMS *Titanic* (RMS stands for Royal Mail Ship). The *Titanic* was the world-famous ocean liner that sank when she struck an iceberg on her maiden (or first) voyage across the Atlantic in 1912. So Mum made herself a huge cardboard ship outfit, complete with a hat that looked like a ship's funnel with smoke coming out of the top.

Ben hated every minute of the dance rehearsals, but he tried his best for his mum. He didn't want to let her down the night she was to dance for her idol Flavio Flavioli or embarrass himself in front of the Queen. However, Ben had always felt that he'd been born with two left feet.

SPOT THE DIFFERENCE

BEN'S RIGHT FOOT

BEN'S LEFT FOOT

Ben wasn't stupid. He knew he was never going to be a great **ballroom-dancing** superstar like Flavio. But he was pretty sure Flavio didn't know how to unblock a toilet. So that seemed fair.

That week, Ben ate, slept and breathed ballroom. His arms ached, his feet were sore, his knees cracked, his head spun and his legs were wibbly wobbly woo-woo from all the dancing. What's more, he'd now heard ♡ "My Heart Will Go On" ♥ at least a hundred times a day. Every time Mum put it back on the stereo, Ben wanted to cover his ears with his sink plungers.

He was almost too exhausted to carry on his detective work, but then the weirdest thing happened...

15

CLUELESS

Sunday was the day Ben always visited Edna. After much pleading with Mum, he was allowed time off rehearsals to see her. Mum rehearsed with a sack of potatoes instead, which was probably a much better dancer than Ben was. That night was the dance competition, so Ben was under strict instructions to be back home by lunchtime.

The boy took pride in performing odd jobs for Edna, particularly anything plumbing-related. He always made a detour on the way to pick up a bag of **Murray Mints** for her.

DING!

"Ah! Ben! My favourite customer!" called out Raj.

"Ah! Raj! My favourite newsagent!" replied the boy. "Thank you for saving my bacon the other day."

"I like nothing more than annoying that annoying Mr Parker."

"Me too!"

"He didn't follow you here today?"

"I don't think so. I sneaked out through the back garden."

"Good thinking. Did you hear? There's been another theft!"

"No!" replied Ben, instantly glowing with guilt, even though he hadn't done a thing.

"Yes. Somebody stole the waxwork of the Queen from Madame Tussauds in the dead of night," replied Raj, holding up the front page of the newspaper.

"Let me see," said Ben, taking the paper.

"There is no free browsing, I'm afraid," said Raj, taking it back.

The World News

QUEEN'S WAXWORK
STOLEN!
POLICE CLUELESS

The waxwork of Her Majesty the Queen was stolen during the night from the world-famous waxwork museum Madame Tussauds in London. Despite the latest high-tech security, the thief managed to evade detection. The motivation for the theft is unknown. No clues were left behind at the scene of the crime to link this theft with those of the mask of Tutankhamun and the World Cup. Although the value of the waxwork is unknown, this is another major embarrassment for the police, who yet again find themselves without a clue.

"The Queen's waxwork? That's a super-weird thing to steal," said Ben.

"Hmm," mused Raj. "Hardly priceless like the mask of Tutankhamun or the **WORLD CUP** or one of my Mr Blobby Easter eggs from 1993."

"No," replied Ben, not at all convinced that an out-of-date Easter egg featuring a big pink blob on the box was a comparable treasure. "If you're going to the trouble of breaking into Madame Tussauds at night, then why steal just the one waxwork? There must be hundreds of dummies of famous people in there! So why just nick the one of the Queen?"

"A prank?"

"Maybe. But the timing, right after the other heists, makes me suspicious. Another daring theft in the dead of night. There must be more to it. I need to do some **detective work!**"

"But, first, your **Murray Mints** for young Miss Edna, sir?"

"Oh yes! Thank you!" said Ben, taking the bag and putting the money down on the counter.

"Where are you going?"

"The waxwork museum, of course!"

"How are you going to get there?"

"Millicent!"

"It would be quicker to walk."

"Ha! Ha! You are right, Raj!"

"Let me give you a ride in the *RAJ RACER!*"

Before long, the pair were cruising through central London and soon arrived at Madame Tussauds.

Raj waited in the car, while Ben sneaked round to the back entrance. Seeing some waxworks being unloaded from a truck into the museum, Ben climbed into the truck and stayed perfectly still. He'd nestled himself between Admiral Nelson and Charlie Chaplin. In moments, the truck driver hoisted Ben up by his legs and carried him into the museum. As soon as Ben had been set down and the lorry driver had plodded off to unload the next waxwork, Ben darted off down the corridor.

He needed to find the scene of the crime, to see if there were any clues the police had missed. Eventually, after passing the waxworks of presidents and popes and pop stars, but strangely no plumbers, he found the room where the figures of the British royal family were on display. As the theft had been in the news, the room was full of tourists eager to catch a glimpse of the empty space where the waxwork of the Queen had stood. Some were even taking pictures of… well, nothing.

Ben looked around the ornate red-and-gold room, decorated to look like the inside of Buckingham Palace. His eyes scanned for possible ways in which the thief might have broken in and made their escape with the Queen's waxwork.

The air vent? Too small to fit through.

A window? There weren't any!

The ceiling? The panels didn't show any signs of being forced.

Ben scoured the deep-red rug on the floor. Maybe the thief had come from below somehow. He noticed the tiniest bump under the corner of the rug. He looked around. Everyone else was focused on the waxworks, so he bent down and lifted up the corner. At first it looked like nothing, just a white square on the wooden floor. It was only when Ben bent down to pick it up that he realised what it was.

A SCRABBLE letter!

Just as Ben straightened up,

he felt a hand on his shoulder.

"Stop right there!"

came a voice.

16

IDENTICAL STRANGERS

When Ben turned round, he saw a tall and wide security guard standing behind him.

"What have you got there?" demanded the lady.

"N-n-nothing!" spluttered Ben.

"If it's nothing, then open your hand."

Ben did as he was told.

"Other hand!" she barked.

This clue was **EXPLOSIVE.** He couldn't surrender it now.

"Oh look! One of the waxworks has come alive!" he shouted, pointing in the opposite direction.

It was enough to make the security

guard turn and look, allowing Ben to make his escape.

"STOP HIM!" shouted the security guard.

But Ben ran and slid under the legs of all the tourists and darted out of the museum the way he'd entered. He leaped into the waiting car.

"DRIVE!" he cried to Raj, and together they sped off as the security guard ran after them.

VROOM!

When they'd lost her, Ben showed Raj his stolen treasure.

"Look!" he said, opening his hand.

"A SCRABBLE letter! So, it must be…"

"THE SAME THIEF!" they said together.

"Where did you find it?"

"Under the rug in the royal room. But it is just a Z ! Before, the SCRABBLE letters spelled out words – what does a Z mean on its own?"

Raj shrugged. "I don't know, but it's ten points if you can use it!"

"Unless the thief just dropped it by mistake!" exclaimed Ben.

"What a clever clog you are, Ben! You could be the new Miss Marble, or Shirley Holmes!"

"Thank you, Raj."

"Where to now, boss?"

Ben checked his watch. "Please can you drop me off at the old folk's home? I was meant to be there half an hour ago and Edna will be getting worried. I don't want her phoning my parents!"

"Of course! Hold on tight!" replied Raj, racing off as fast as a Reliant Robin can go.

VROOM!

"Interesting. Very interesting, dear," was Edna's verdict as she examined the SCRABBLE piece in her little bedroom over tea and **Murray Mints.**

Ben loved visiting Edna. They would often talk about Granny, and Edna would get out her old leather-bound photo album, which had pictures of the two close cousins from the olden days. However, today Ben wanted to show her what he'd found. He didn't want the old lady to worry so had told her as little as possible, but Edna was a wise old bird. She followed the news like a hawk and knew that the boy's discovery had something to do with the heists.

"It's just a SCRABBLE letter," said Ben with a shrug.

"It's not 'just' anything, dear."

"But there must be millions of these SCRABBLE pieces in the world, if not billions!"

"Fetch me the SCRABBLE set on the side, would you, dear?" she asked.

"We'd better not get the pieces mixed up. I need to pass this one on to the police."

"Of course. But all in good time."

Ben fetched the dusty old SCRABBLE box. "Granny's old set. It still smells of cabbage," he said, having a sniff of the box.

"I would have preferred your granny to have left me her mobility scooter, but there you go!"

"Sorry, Edna!" replied Ben with a chuckle. "I do miss her so much."

"Of course you do. But she's right there in your heart, isn't she?" she said, patting the boy on his chest.

"Yep. Always will be."

The old lady smiled and opened the box. Carefully she picked up the bag of letters.

CLINK! CLINK! CLINK! went the letters as they clinked into each other. Next, she poured them out of the bag and laid them down on the coffee table.

"Now where's the Z ?" she asked herself.

"There it is, Edna!" replied Ben, pointing.

"Very good, dear. Now, you lay your Z next to mine."

Ben did just that, placing his letter down on the coffee table.

"I can't see any difference!" he exclaimed. "Z . Ten points."

"Look again, dear!" said Edna, shaking her head

at the boy's impatience.

Ben studied the two pieces. "Well, they are very slightly different colours."

"Very good."

"Granny's old one is white, while this one is cream. Like ivory."

"That's what I saw, dear! And my eyes aren't what they were. Let's do a tap test."

"A what?"

"You tap yours on the table first, and then I will tap mine."

"But why?"

"Just trust me!"

Ben shook his head, and then tapped the piece on the wooden table.

THONK!

Next Edna tapped hers.

THUNK!

"Different sounds!" exclaimed Ben. "But they look pretty much identical."

"Identical strangers!" replied Edna. "They must be

made of different things. My piece is plastic, but your one…"

Ben tapped his on the table again.

THONK!

"…is bone china!"

"Bone china? I thought all the pieces in a SCRABBLE set were made of plastic."

"So did I. But the one you found at the scene of the crime must be from a specially made SCRABBLE set."

"Who has a SCRABBLE set made specially for them?"

"I don't have all the answers, Ben, but I think you have your first

major clue!"

17

Ben kept the clue safely clenched in the palm of his hand. He didn't dare put the SCRABBLE piece in his pocket in case it bounced out.

This clue was DYNAMITE! It linked the thief to all three crimes! Ben would hand it over to the police, and then, surely, they could do the rest. Fingerprints. DNA samples. Finding out who in the world had a special SCRABBLE set with letters made of china. Once the police arrested the real culprit, Mr Parker and his army of oldies would be off Ben's back forever. The boy would be proved innocent. Phew!

Ben glanced down at his hand to check the SCRABBLE piece was still there. Not looking where he was going, he walked SLAP BANG into a metal bin.

BOINK!

DISASTER! The SCRABBLE piece slipped from his hand.

CLINK!

This was no ordinary metal bin. This one had a man inside. **Mr Parker, of course!**

This metal bin was the latest disguise of Ben's arch-enemy.

He'd cut away the bottom of the bin so his legs were showing. His face was peeking out of the gap between the bin and the lid.

"Mr Parker!" said the boy from the ground.

The man in the bin stood over him menacingly.

"Your friendly Neighbourhood Watch group leader, Lower Toddle branch!" he sneered. "Where have you been?"

"Nowhere," replied Ben.

"You must have been somewhere."

"No, Mr Parker! I haven't been anywhere!"

"Thought you could outsmart me in the car park, did you?"

HOW TO DISGUISE YOURSELF AS A BIN:

Find a friendly bin.

Give it a wipe.

Give it one more wipe, just to be sure.

Give it another wipe.

Attach the lid to your head by a chin strap.

Attach shoulder straps to the inside of the bin.

Climb inside the bin.

Cut off the bottom of the bin.

Stand up and take the weight of the bin on your shoulders.

CONGRATULATIONS! YOU ARE A BIN!

"No. I'm sorry. I just—"

"No one outsmarts Mr Parker! Or my **Neighbourhood Watch** army!"

Just then all the bins on the street came alive. Wheelie bins. Recycling bins. Compost bins. Every type of bin imaginable had one of his oldies in it.

In a pincer movement, they soon had Ben surrounded.

"I haven't done anything wrong!" protested the boy.

"I will be the judge of that!" replied Mr Parker.

"Throw the book at him!" said his sister, who was disguised as a compost bin.

"Lock him up and throw away the key!" added a little pedal bin at the back.

"And what is that lying on the ground?" demanded Mr Parker, his red eyes narrowing.

"Me?" asked Ben, who was indeed still lying on the ground.

"No!" snarled Mr Parker, bending down with great difficulty – as well you might, if you were disguised as a bin. "THIS!"

The nosy neighbour held the SCRABBLE piece aloft as if he'd just found the Holy Grail.

"I can explain!" spluttered Ben.

"You can explain everything to the police, as that is where we are taking you right now!"

From the pavement, Ben looked all around. A bin was approaching from every angle.

Just as he was about to give up hope, he saw a shape hopping from branch to branch in the tree above.

It was the **black cat!**

The cat looked straight at Ben. Ben stared back.

"What are you looking at?" demanded Miss Parker, looming over her brother's shoulder.

Ben was sure that the cat was up to something.

"Nothing!" he chirped, mock-innocently.

Just as he hoped, the cat leaped down from the tree.

WHOOSH!

It landed on the back of Miss Parker's bin.

CLONK!

"ARGH!" she cried as she fell forward on to her brother.

CLONK!

"OOOHHH!"

Both began falling, so Ben rolled out of the way.

The pair crashed on to the ground.

KERUNCH!

The force of the blow sent the SCRABBLE piece flying through the air.

The cat caught it in its mouth, and then put it in Ben's hand.

"Thanks!" he said. "You've got my back, haven't you?"

"MIAOW!" miaowed the cat, though Ben wasn't sure if it was a yes or a no.

154

There wasn't time to hang about to find out, as the army of bins was forming a circle round him.

"You are trapped!" shouted Mr Parker as Ben wriggled around on the ground desperately trying to get up.

"I don't think so!" said Ben.

With that, he rolled Mr Parker towards the other bins.

TRUNDLE!

It knocked them over like skittles!

THONK! THONK! THONK!

Now Ben had an escape route. Clutching the SCRABBLE piece in his hand, he ran home as fast as he could, the bins chasing him all the way.

"STOP HIM!"

"SEIZE THAT BOY!"

"LOCK HIM UP AND THROW AWAY THE KEY!"

The cat used its tail to trip one of them up.

THONK!

But they kept on coming.

When he turned the corner into his street, Ben spotted his parents waiting outside the house with a pair of suitcases.

"BEN! WHERE ON EARTH HAVE YOU BEEN?" shouted Mum. "WE'RE GOING TO BE LATE FOR THE DANCE COMPETITION!"

"START THE CAR!" called Ben as the army of bins loomed behind him.

"WHAT?" shouted Dad.

"START THE CAR! NOW!"

Mum and Dad stuffed the bags in the boot and jumped into their little brown car.

The car sped out of the drive. Ben dived in through the passenger window, his legs still waggling as the car zoomed away.

VROOOM!

18

A DEEP SENSE
OF
DREAD

As Ben saw the huge dome of the Royal Albert Hall come into view, he felt a deep sense of dread in his tummy.

It must seat thousands of people, thought Ben. He couldn't believe he'd ever agreed to perform there! Especially not in front of the Queen!

"Dad, how's your knee?" he asked as he hid the SCRABBLE piece down his underpants.

"Oh! That's kind of you to ask, son. It's a tiny bit better," replied Dad.

"A tiny bit better! It's a MIRACLE!"

"You what?"

"You will dance in front of the Queen!"

"Oh no, Benjamin!" snapped Mum. "You are not getting out of it that easily!"

"But—" protested Ben.

"I know what you are trying to do. No. No. No. This is so much more original! Ben, don't you realise that we're about to make HISTORY?"

"It's not exactly World War Two," retorted Ben.

"BALLROOM-DANCING HISTORY! The mother-and-son dance sensation soon to take over the world!"

"I was thinking of retiring after tonight," he replied.

"Retiring? This is just the beginning. Tonight, a ballroom legend will be born!"

It's official! thought Ben. *My mum is bonkers!*

Once inside the Royal Albert Hall, Dad said, "Break a leg," as he took his seat in the auditorium. This is what showbusiness people say to wish each other good luck on the stage, but it seemed wrong to say it now as there was a very real possibility someone's leg *would* get broken.

Meanwhile, Ben and Mum were taken backstage into a huge dressing room by one of the organisers. It was bursting with ballroom couples preening themselves in front of the lit mirrors. They all seemed to know each other well and greeted each other in a fake-friendly way by kissing the air and calling each other "darling".

"Mwah! Mwah!"

"Do tell me the shade of your fake tan, darling! Or did you use brown sauce?"

"You are so brave wearing yellow with a

bottom as big as that, my dear!"

"I do hope you don't twist your ankle like last time, darling!"

"*Your hair is a wonder, darling! Is it a wig?*"

"Still dancing at your age, darling! You are an inspiration!"

The pair put on their costumes, Ben his iceberg outfit, and Mum her *Titanic* outfit. There were titters from the other dancers.

His mother tried to touch up her inch-thick make-up in the mirror as the other competitors were elbowing her out of the way, and Ben began wishing for something, anything, that could save him...

 Could the Royal Albert Hall turn out to be a flying saucer and zoom off into the sky?

Or could London be swept away by a *tidal wave* of custard?

 How about a superhero and a supervillain deciding to have a super-fight in London and destroying the Royal Albert Hall?

Perhaps one of the tap dancers could tap too hard on the stage and cause the Royal Albert Hall to **crumble** to the ground?

What if Ben ate a *magic* sugar cube and shrank to the size of a Jelly Baby so he could run away?

Or a giant might rip off the roof of the Royal Albert Hall and devour all the dancers?

What if Britain were attacked by giant killer tomatoes?

Or a hole in the space-time continuum opened and **DINOSAURS** returned to stalk the Earth? Perhaps a *Tyrannosaurus rex* might be kind enough to gobble down Ben's mother? Especially if Ben asked politely.

If only a **giant meteor** would tumble through space and land directly on the Royal Albert Hall! That would be A FANTASTIC STROKE OF GOOD LUCK!

Or an army of **billions** of hungry ants could devour the Royal Albert Hall brick by brick in seconds?

Sadly, despite Ben's prayers, none of the above happened.

Instead, a voice over the intercom said, "Ben and Linda Herbert to the stage, please!"

What could possibly go wrong?

As it turned out, absolutely

everything...

19

PLUCKED TO PERFECTION

Standing in the darkness just off to the side of the vast stage, Ben and his mum waited for Flavio Flavioli to announce their names.

"*Your Royal Majestical Majesty Highness the Queen,*" began Flavio as he stood in the place he clearly loved the most: the spotlight. As usual, the **ballroom-dancing** TV star was waxed, buffed, sprayed, oiled and plucked to perfection.

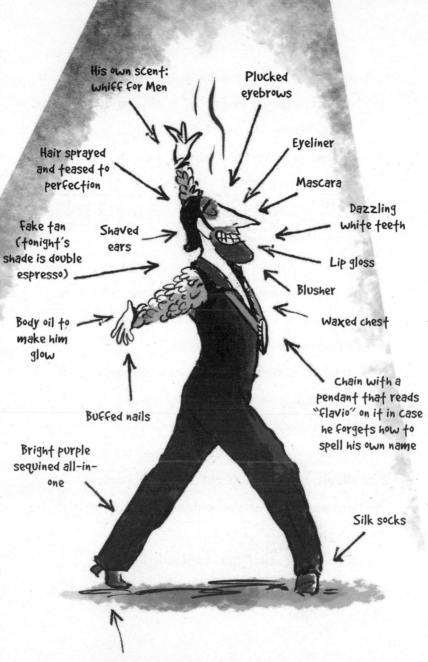

Ben stood there, blinking in the wings. The lights on the stage were so bright he could barely keep his eyes open. There was a one-hundred-piece orchestra at the back, all shuffling through their sheet music to find the next piece to play.

"Ladies and gentlemen, boys and girls, it gives me great pleasure to introduce our next competitors to the stage. They are a mother-and-son ballroom couple…"

There were murmurs of surprise from the audience. This was something they'd never seen before, and most likely would never see again!

"…and their names are Ben and Linda Herbert. I imagine that Ben is the son and Linda is the mother. They have come all the way from the Outer Hebrides to be with us, where I am told they are huge stars. For our competition tonight, they will present to you the dramatic story of the sinking of the *Titanic*… in DANCE!"

Those in the audience applauded politely, except for Dad, who was alone in bouncing to his feet and cheering wildly.

"HURRAH!"

As all eyes turned to him, Dad's face contorted in pain.

"OOH! ME KNEE!" he cried, toppling backwards on to his seat.

DOOF!

Meanwhile, Linda leaped on to the stage, dragging a reluctant Ben along with her. The applause turned to laughter when everyone saw their funny costumes. It had been a night of absurd attire, but a ship and an **iceberg** were off-the-scale NUTS!

"HA! HA! HA!"

Ben would have been happy for the world to end if that meant he didn't have to stand on the stage for a moment longer. He did his best to hide behind his mother, but the iceberg outfit was so big and bulky that it was impossible not to be seen. It was farcical, and made the audience laugh even more.

"HA! HA! HA!"

Just wait until you see us dance, thought Ben. *Then you are really going to laugh!*

Mum's lip curled and her nose wrinkled, but Ben kept his head down. He didn't want the Queen to recognise him from that night with Granny at the Tower of London.

Fortunately, the Queen was a long way from the stage, sitting high up in the royal box.

Flavio was much nearer. He instantly recognised the pair. How could he forget the night when Ben danced solo in the junior ballroom competition and scored the lowest marks ever recorded in the entire world?

Three zeroes.

Even when you added up all the scores, they still made zero.

A BIG FAT ZERO!

However, the person who alarmed Flavio the most, judging by the look of horror on his face, was Mum.

This was the superfan who had rushed to give him mouth-to-mouth resuscitation when he'd been hit on the head by a tap shoe!

"Oh no. It's you!" said Flavio under his breath, as Linda got uncomfortably close to him.

"Oh yes!" she replied. "It's me! And look at my nails."

She whisked her hands in front of his face. As Mum worked in a nail salon, she was always coming home with weird and wonderful creations on the ends of her fingers. Tonight, her nails spelled out: I LOVE FLAVI

"If I had another finger, I would have been able to include the O!" she explained.

Flavio smiled weakly, shook his head and cha-cha-cha-ed away from this superfan as fast as he could.

Just before he disappeared from view, Flavio brought the microphone back up to his mouth: "MUSIC, PLEASE!"

The elderly conductor tapped his baton on his lectern and the orchestra started playing the world-famous theme tune from the film *Titanic*,

"My Heart Will Go On".

20

Just as they'd rehearsed, RMS *Titanic* (Mum) and the iceberg (Ben) circled each other on the stage as the music boomed. Next, they came together and mirrored each other's movements before Ben took his mother by the hand and they began to waltz around the stage. The boy was short for his age and the height difference looked a little silly. There were chuckles from the audience, before there was the loud sound of someone shushing.

"SHUSH!"

It was Dad, proudly defending his family's honour by urging the 5,271 other people in the Royal Albert Hall to be quiet.

Then came the first dramatic dance move of the routine. With some difficulty, the RMS *Titanic* hoisted the iceberg up and placed him on top of her head. Next, she spun round on the spot as Ben stretched out his arms and legs like a starfish and prayed that nobody from his school happened to be in the audience.

What followed was a daring manoeuvre, which Mum was sure would wow the judges. Holding on to Ben's ankles, she let him slide down her back to the stage. Despite being short for his age, the boy was on the heavy side. He slumped down to the floor with a **THUMP.**

"HA! HA! HA!" chuckled the audience.

"Careful, Mum!" hissed Ben.

"I am the *Titanic*, thank you very much, Ben, I mean… the iceberg!" she hissed back.

Then she grabbed her son by his ankles.

"Ouch! Mind your nails!" he moaned as her false nails dug into his skin.

"Shush!" snapped Mum.

Once she had a good grip on him, she dragged Ben by the ankles across the stage, spinning him round on his back. If you'd just walked into the Royal Albert Hall, you would be forgiven for thinking that the lady was using the boy to clean the floor.

But no sooner had this part of the routine started than a new one began. As the song moved towards its dramatic crescendo, the *Titanic* let go of the iceberg. The iceberg rolled over and scrambled to his feet, before pacing over to the *Titanic* who stood still, centre stage.

"I'm not sure I can do the spin!" whispered Ben.

"It's the big finish!"

"I'll do my best!"

"For Flavio!"

Against his better judgement, Ben took his mother by the wrists. Instantly, he could feel her nails dig deep into his skin again.

"OUCH!"

"Shush!" she shushed.

Then he began spinning her.

Slowly at first, and then as the music gathered momentum so did Mum.

Her feet lifted off the ground as she was whirled round in the air.

The audience seemed impressed by this. It was not every day you saw a boy lift his own mother off the ground.

There was a smattering of applause, and a shout of encouragement from Dad.

"THIS IS DYNAMITE!"

Ben grimaced at the pain of Mum's nails digging into his arms.

"This is agony!" he moaned.

"Don't let go!" pleaded Mum.

WHIRR!

Now she'd taken on a momentum all of her own. As much as he wanted to, Ben just couldn't stop spinning his mother round. She was going so fast it was impossible to slow down.

WHIRR!

The faster she spun, the more Mum's nails dug into Ben's skin. His eyes were watering with the pain.

"MUM! I can't hold you any longer!" he cried.

"Of course you can! The routine is nearly over! Just a few seconds more!"

"I CAN'T! HELP! SOMEONE, PLEASE HELP!"

WHIRR!

WHIRR!

The conductor of the orchestra didn't know what to do and began conducting faster and faster. This made the music speed up. As the song whirled out of control, so did Mum.

WHIRR!

Her nails were dragging across Ben's arms and hands.

Flavio Flavioli watched on from the side of the

stage, aghast at what he saw.

"FLAVIO! SAVE ME!" called out Mum as her feet skimmed his hair.

Flavio dodged out of the way. In desperation he ran across the stage, hoping to avoid being hit.

How wrong he was.

"I AM SORRY, MUM!" called Ben as her fingers slipped out of his.

WHOOSH!

"CALL ME *TITANIC!*" she cried as she zoomed through the air. Mum was going so fast she was little more than a blur. A blur that hit Flavio so hard…

BOOMF!

…that he was sent flying into the auditorium.

Flavio landed right on Dad.

CRUMP!

Just as Mum came to a stop upside down on top of the judges in the front row, "My Heart Will Go On" ♥ reached its soaring conclusion! ♥ ♥

Then there was a deep silence,

broken only by Ben saying,

"Oops!"

21

BROKEN BUTTOCK

"I think one of my buttocks is broken!" moaned Flavio.

"Not your buttock! Noooooo!" cried Mum.

"Me other knee has gone now too!" whimpered Dad.

From the side of the stage, a tap shoe flew through the air.

WHIZZ!

It struck Ben on the back of his head.

"OUCH!"

He toppled over into the orchestra pit...

DOOF!

...landing on the conductor.

DOOF!

In turn, the conductor tumbled forward on to his lectern.

THWACK!

It was only the beginning of a giant domino topple, involving the entire orchestra!

The lectern toppled on to the harpist.

BASH!

The harp collapsed on top of the violinists.

TWANG!

Who in turn fell on to the brass section.

TOOT!

The brass section fell on to the pianist.

KERTHUNK!

The grand piano shot forward and rammed into the drums.

BANG!

Soon all the musicians and their instruments were a swirling mass in the orchestra pit.

Suddenly, the outraged audience members leaped from their seats, pointing at Ben.

"That boy has ruined tonight!"

"It's all his fault!"

"THIS IS AN OUTRAGE!"

"He must pay!"

"WICKED CHILD!"

"Stop that boy!"

"GET HIM!"

"Grab him by the ice cubes!"

"PUT HIM UNDER ARREST!"

"Melt him down to a puddle!"

Ben clambered out of the pit back up on to the stage, but soon a circle of police officers who were there to protect the Queen had surrounded him.

The boy made a run for it. He leaped off the stage and on to the back of one of the audience's chairs. As a sea of hands struggled to grab him by the ankles, he sprang from seat to seat.

BOING!

BOING!

BOING!

But soon everywhere he looked there was NO WAY OUT!

In desperation, Ben looked up at the royal box. Maybe the Queen would protect him? So he hurdled over the chairs and threw himself at the boxes that walled the auditorium. It was hard going dressed as an iceberg, but soon Ben had climbed up to the royal box. He hoisted himself over the balcony and then fell on to the floor and flapped around like a caught fish.

Ben clambered to his knees and stayed there. He was more than happy to grovel.

"Your Majesty," he began, "I don't know if you remember me. I am Ben. I met you late one night with my granny in the Tower of London. We were there to steal the *Crown Jewels*. You kindly pardoned me that night, and tonight I throw myself at your feet. Please! I beg you, help me!"

He looked up, but the Queen's expression did not change.

Below there was a storm of outrage.

"WHAT DO YOU THINK YOU ARE DOING, BOY?"

"STEP AWAY FROM HER MAJESTY THE QUEEN!"

"LOCK HIM UP IN THE TOWER!"

In desperation, Ben reached out his hand to touch the Queen's.

"PLEASE!"

At that moment, he noticed something strange.

The Queen's hand was cold to the touch.

In an instant, Ben realised

that this wasn't the Queen!

It was her

waxwork!

22

A MYSTERIOUS FIGURE

B{\scriptsize ANG}! B{\scriptsize ANG}! **B{\scriptsize ANG}!**

There was pounding on the door of the royal box.

"OPEN UP! POLICE!"

Ben's heart was pounding too. He leaped into the box next door, which was full of posh people in dinner suits and ball gowns.

"Excuse me!" he said as he rushed past them and out of the door.

Ben glanced to his right to see an army of police outside the royal box.

The police officers all stared at him. Ben smiled back, before saying, "Good evening." Then he began slowly sliding away so as not to arouse suspicion. However, being dressed as a giant block of ice did make him rather conspicuous.

The police officers all nodded back before the least dense one recognised him.

"It's the iceberg boy!" he cried. "After him!"

Ben sprinted along the circular hallway to escape. Up ahead, he saw a *mysterious* figure disappear through a door with a sign on it that read:

NO ENTRY

Glancing over his shoulder, Ben saw that he was just out of sight of the police, so he snuck through the door and shut it tight behind him. He loitered in the darkness as he heard footsteps run past. Ben had lost them. For now. Some way ahead, he saw a shaft of light appear and disappear as the figure passed through another door. He raced along the narrow corridor to catch up. When he opened the next door, he saw an old spiral staircase up which the figure was now racing.

CLUNK! CLUNK! CLUNK!

The boy kept his distance – he didn't want this figure to spot him. So he waited until the person had reached the top before he clunked up the stairs too.

CLUNK! CLUNK! CLUNK!

At the top of the spiral staircase was a hatch. When Ben opened it, he found himself on the domed roof of the Royal Albert Hall.

Standing right at the top of the dome was the figure.

The figure had whipped off their clothes and was now wearing an all-in-one black jumpsuit, just like the one Ben's granny had worn as **THE BLACK CAT!** Then the figure produced a mask and put it over their head.

Next, they pulled a cord on their bag.

YANK!

Instantly, the most incredible thing happened! Like some high-tech gadget, the bag transformed in seconds into... a hang-glider!

SCHWOOM!

The figure then got into position on the hang-glider. But before Ben could cry out, "WHO ARE YOU?"

they took a run-up and launched into

the night sky.

WHOOSH!

23

GIANT MUSHROOMS

"STOP RIGHT THERE!" came a shout from behind.

Ben turned round and saw the police standing on the domed roof of the Royal Albert Hall.

In the night sky, the *mysterious* figure was fluttering away on their hang-glider into the distance. Ben was sure there had to be some advantage to being dressed as an iceberg. So, without a word, he ran towards the police. On seeing this great lump of cardboard ice hurtling towards them, they leaped out of the way.

"ARGH!"

"HELP!"

"NOO!"

They toppled over and slid down the sides of the dome as Ben made his escape. The door he'd come through was now blocked by more police officers, but luckily he found a hatch on the roof, which he managed to bust open.

BAM!

Unluckily, it led straight into the auditorium. It was a VERY LONG WAY DOWN!

Dangling from the ceiling of the Royal Albert Hall were a large number of what looked like giant mushrooms. They were made of fibreglass and were there to stop sound echoing around the auditorium. As the police swarmed towards the hatch, Ben felt he had no choice. He leaped down and landed on one of the giant mushrooms.

DOINK!

Because it was dangling from wires, the mushroom on which Ben had landed began to swing, clonking into all the others.

CLONK! CLONK!

Ben leaped from mushroom to mushroom as the thousands of people below looked on, aghast.

"GASP!"

"DON'T FALL, BEN!" Dad shouted up.

"I WASN'T PLANNING TO!" Ben shouted down.

Soon he'd clonked his way to the side of the hall. He leaped off the last mushroom and made his escape along the passageways and down the staircases.

However, in every direction Ben ran, there were more and more police. There was no way he could barge through them now. They were forming human walls by linking arms together as they would do to control a crowd.

"WE HAVE YOU TRAPPED, BOY! STOP THIS NONSENSE AND GIVE YOURSELF UP!" shouted one police officer who looked more senior than the rest.

To Ben's side a window opened.

CREAK!

It was being pushed open by the **black cat!**

It nudged the pane of glass with its head. Ben winked at the cat. It purred and blinked back at him.

"PURR!"

The creature had saved him once again. The window was his only way of escape. Despite still being dressed as an iceberg, he replied to the police with a heroic, "NEVER!"

Then, waiting until the exact moment that an open-top sightseeing bus slowed down outside the hall, he made a leap.

WHOOSH!

THUMP!

He landed on his bottom on the back seat of the bus, which immediately moved off.

VROOM!

Ben allowed himself a little wave at the police officers all gathered at the window.

"BYE!" he called out.

Next, he searched the skies for a sign of the mysterious figure.

Far off in the distance, he could just make out the shape of their hang-glider silhouetted against the moon. But the bus he was sitting on was heading the wrong way! So he pressed the bell, rushed down the spiral stairs and got off. Fortunately, another London sightseeing bus was travelling in the opposite direction. Ben crossed the road and boarded that one, racing up to the top deck.

Once again, he searched the skies until he spotted the hang-glider.

It soared over the River Thames and through Tower Bridge. The figure landed on the roof of one of the most famous historic buildings in the world.

The Tower of London.

Ben's brain buzzed.

Was someone about to steal the *Crown Jewels?*

24

Ben climbed up on to a bin so he could stand on the high stone wall that ringed the Tower of London. He looked at the medieval castle lit up at night. He hadn't been here since the night he and Granny had tried to steal the *Crown Jewels*.

Ben crossed the moat and scaled the second wall. Next, he jumped down into the grounds, and tiptoed over to Waterloo Block, in which lay the Jewel House.

The castle on the River Thames is home to some magnificent buildings. There is:

THE CHAPEL ROYAL OF ST PETER AD VINCULA
Translated from the Latin, this means "St Peter in Chains".
It is the burial place of some of the most famous prisoners
executed at the Tower, such as one of King Henry VIII's
more unfortunate wives, Anne Boleyn.

WATERLOO BLOCK
Once a barracks, the block is now home
to the Jewel House. This is the vault
where the Crown Jewels are kept.

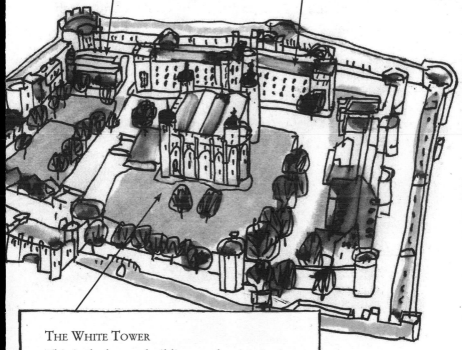

THE WHITE TOWER
This is the largest building on the site. It gives
the Tower of London its name and is famous
for being a prison from 1100 to 1952.

The Tower of London was patrolled by Yeoman Warders or Beefeaters. They were nicknamed "Beefeaters" as legend has it they were paid in beef! They were instantly recognisable because they had:

Tudor bonnet

Military medals

White neck ruff

Scarlet-and-gold tunic

The initials E.R. on their tunic: this stands for Elizabeth Regina (Regina being the Latin word for Queen)

White gloves

The thistle, rose and shamrock on their chest: these are the emblems of Scotland, England and Ireland

Lantern

Stockings

Ribbons on their shoes

Knee breeches

Pole (a medieval weapon)

Traditionally, these old soldiers have the task of keeping the *Crown Jewels* safe for the monarch.

Despite still being dressed as an iceberg, Ben managed to stick to the shadows to avoid being detected. Just as he reached the Jewel House, he heard the Beefeaters exchanging words with each other.

"Halt! Who comes there?"

"The keys."

"Whose keys?"

"Queen Elizabeth's keys."

"Pass, Queen Elizabeth's keys. All's well."

Next Ben heard feet marching on the cobblestones…

STOMP! STOMP! STOMP!

…before the voices called out to each other again: "God preserve Queen Elizabeth."

"Amen!"

There followed the sound of the clock striking ten times.

BONG! BONG! BONG! BONG! BONG! BONG! BONG! BONG! BONG! BONG!

Ben looked up at the Jewel House. The *mysterious* figure had scaled down the building and was now forcing open a window. Whoever they were, they'd timed it perfectly! They had used the Beefeaters' "Ceremony of the Keys", which takes place every night just before ten o'clock, as a distraction.

Ben tiptoed over to the Jewel House and climbed up the drainpipe to the window the figure had forced

open. Once inside, he made his way down the stone steps to the ground floor where the *Crown Jewels* were on display.

The masked figure was standing over the thick glass case that houses the *Crown Jewels*, holding a stick of dynamite. Dynamite was the only thing that had a chance of breaking through that glass. The figure must be trying to steal them!

There are many *Crown Jewels,* but the most celebrated are:

THE SOVEREIGN'S SCEPTRE

The Sovereign's Sceptre symbolises the power of the monarch. It is decorated with the Great Star of Africa, the largest clear-cut diamond in the world.

ST EDWARD'S CROWN

This is named after Edward the Confessor, the King of England from 1042 to 1066 who was immortalised in the Bayeux Tapestry. The heavy crown is decorated with 444 precious stones. These include amethysts, garnets, peridots, rubies, sapphires, topazes, tourmalines and zircons.

THE SOVEREIGN'S ORB

Sovereign is another name for king or queen, and the orb represents the Earth. It is as if the monarch is holding the entire world in their hand. It is made of gold, sapphires, rubies, emeralds, amethysts, diamonds, pearls and enamel. It has been used at all coronations since Charles II's in 1661.

Bong!

Ben watched in horror as the figure lit the fuse on the stick of dynamite.

SIZZLE!

In just a few moments, it was going to explode!

As they placed it down on the glass, Ben called out from the shadows, "Please don't!"

"Who goes there?"

Ben would recognise that voice anywhere.

It was *Her Majesty the Queen!*

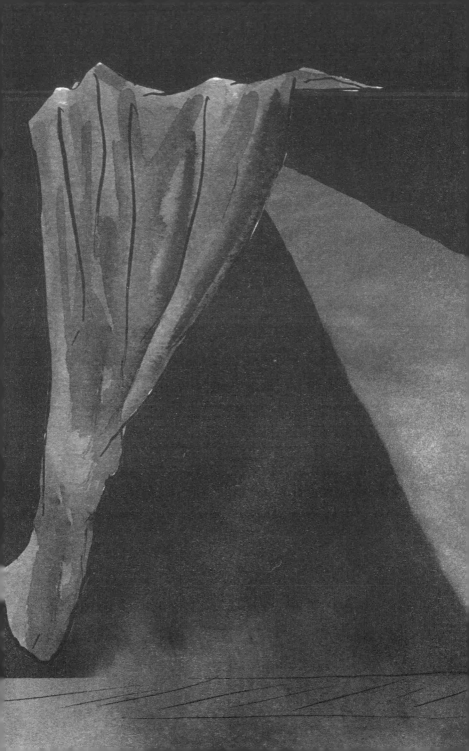

PART THREE
_____

THE SECRET
OF ALL
SECRETS

25

DYNAMITE!

"HALT! WHO GOES THERE?" demanded the Queen again as she turned round and lifted off her mask.

Ben stepped out of the shadows, his whole body wobbling with shock. Why on earth would the Queen want to steal her own *Crown Jewels?* This was BEYOND BONKERS!

"It's m-m-me, Your M-M-Majesty – Ben," he spluttered. "You m-m-met me in this very room a year ago with my g-g-granny."

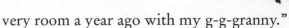

"So one did," replied the Queen haughtily. "One pardoned you both that night. You thought you would come back another night to try your luck, did you? And why on earth are you dressed as an iceberg?"

SIZZLE!

"Your Majesty! The stick of dynamite!"

The Queen looked at the fuse burning away. "Oh fiddlesticks!" she exclaimed. Then she began blowing on the fuse again and again and again.

WUFT! WUFT! WUFT!

"It won't go out! HELP!"

SIZZLE!

Ben rushed over and began blowing too.

WUFT! WUFT! WUFT!

But, however hard they blew, it just wouldn't go out.

"What is one going to do?" exclaimed the Queen.

"Throw it out of the window?" suggested Ben. "Follow me!"

The pair raced back up the stairs to the open window.

The Queen was just about to hurl the stick of dynamite out when she looked down and spotted her guards below.

"One's Beefeaters!" she hissed.

"Other window!" suggested Ben.

SIZZLE!

He ran to another window on the opposite side of the Jewel House, but when the Queen looked out of it she cried, "Ravens!"

"Ravens?"

The boy looked down at the little aviary where the distinctive black birds were sleeping.

"One can't blow up one's own ravens!"

"No! But if you don't throw it somewhere soon you are going to blow *us* up!"

SIZZLE!

They rushed to another side of the building and opened a window. Beyond it was a tall tree.

"Throw it! Now!" begged Ben.

SIZZLE!

The Queen looked out of the window. "There's a

baby squirrel in that tree! Look! One couldn't live with oneself!"

"You are not going to have to live with yourself at this rate!"

SIZZLE!

There was one final side of the building to try. Ben opened the last window and the Queen looked down.

"All clear?" asked Ben.

Sadly, Her Majesty was not convinced. "That's the gift shop!"

"It's midnight! There's no one there!"

"No, but spare a thought for all those Tower of London pencil cases, posable Beefeater action figures and overpriced tins of shortbread with one's face on them!"

"Give it here!" barked Ben. With that, he grabbed the stick of dynamite out of the Queen's hand. "If I remember rightly, there is an old privy in the cellar."

"How do you know that?"

'PLUMBING WEEKLY! Have you ever read it?"

"One can't say one has had the pleasure," replied the Queen, unsurprisingly.

"They did a great 'Toilets Through the Ages' special bumper issue!"

"Oh! One must read that," she said, sounding not at all convinced.

SIZZLE!

The fuse on the stick of dynamite had very nearly run out. There could only be seconds to go.

"You'd best take cover, ma'am!"

"Thank you. But it's ma'am as in 'ham', not ma'am as in 'farm'!"

"Right now, I don't care!" cried Ben as he raced down the steps and found the old toilet underground. The Queen trailed not far behind him.

FIZZLE!

There was a sign on the wooden door that read YE OLDE PRIVY.

Ben threw the stick of dynamite down the ancient toilet and yanked on the chain as hard as he could.

FLUSH!

After a second or two, there was the thunderous sound of an explosion underground.

#

26

Bog water exploded all over Ben.

SPLOOSH!

He was covered from head to toe in it, as if he couldn't look any more ridiculous.

"HA! HA! HA!" laughed the Queen.

"Oh! I get it! So being soaked in bog water is funny, is it?" huffed Ben.

"Well yes, it is rather! Ha! Ha! Ha!"

The lady's laughter was infectious, and in no time Ben was laughing too. "Ha! Ha! Ha!"

"HA! HA! HA! What japes!" she exclaimed. "Goodness knows what one's Beefeaters will make of that awful noise!"

"Maybe they will think someone had a really explosive number two!"

"HA! HA! After a very spicy state banquet," she joined in.

"Ha! Ha! I never knew you were funny!"

"There's an awful lot you don't know about one, young man."

"Clearly! I am absolutely shocked to see you here. Why were you stealing your own *Crown Jewels?*"

"One asked a question first," she replied.

"Did you?"

"Yes. One did. Why are you dressed like an iceberg?"

"Oh right. Yes, you did. I was taking part in the **ballroom-dancing** competition."

"One must have sneaked off just before you came on."

"My mum was the *Titanic*!"

"Goodness gracious!" she exclaimed. "One has had to sit through some rubbish in one's time, but a **ballroom-dancing** piece about the sinking of the *Titanic* takes first prize!"

"So you sneaked off, leaving your own waxwork in your place!"

"How on earth do you know about the waxwork?"

"I climbed up into the royal box!"

"Oh no. Being at the dance competition was meant to be the perfect alibi. One couldn't be in two places at once – the Royal Albert Hall *and* the Tower of London. So no one was going to suspect one!"

Ben was piecing the whole thing together in his mind.

"So, YOU must be behind all these thefts? Tutankhamun's mask, the **WORLD CUP** and, of course, your own waxwork!"

"How do you know one was behind the other thefts?" demanded the Queen. "Out with it, boy!"

"Look!" said Ben, showing her the SCRABBLE piece. "I found this at Madame Tussauds!"

"URGH!" gasped the Queen.

"Don't worry. The police missed it."

"One wondered where one had dropped the Z! As a little tease, one was going to leave behind this little clue here until you barged in!" She pulled out some SCRABBLE letters and arranged them on the table.

HISS

"They are special china pieces, aren't they?" asked Ben.

"SCRABBLE gifted one a bespoke set for one's Silver Jubilee!"

"The pieces for us normal folk are made of plastic!"

The Queen's face turned white with fear. "Really?"

"Yep!"

"Oh no. No. No. No. One hadn't realised. One has rather given the game away, hasn't one?"

"Rather!"

"But the police can't have figured out that one is the owner of the SCRABBLE set."

"No. Not yet!"

"Oh no. If they do, then one is in deep doo-doo."

"The deepest."

The Queen took a breath before uttering, "One needs to put things right."

"Can I ask a question?" asked Ben.

"It isn't normally permitted to ask the monarch a direct question, but on this occasion one will allow it," replied the Queen haughtily.

"Why are you dressed up just like my granny?" asked Ben.

The Queen suddenly looked thrilled. "One must confess that one 'borrowed' your grandmother's delicious idea of having a secret identity! One desperately wanted to be **THE BLACK CAT** too. By the way, where is your grandmother tonight?"

A look of sadness descended on Ben's face. Instantly, the Queen knew what this meant. Granny was gone.

"One is so sorry, Ben," began the Queen.

"Me too," replied Ben.

"One could sense your grandmother really loved you."

"And I loved her."

"All that will remain of us is love," said the Queen.

"Even you?"

"Even one."

"But you're a Queen!"

"THE Queen!" she corrected mock-grandly, with a twinkle of mischief in her eye.

"But you're THE Queen!" said Ben.

"That's better! All that really matters in life is that you give love and are loved in return. It doesn't matter if you are a prince or a pauper."

"Me and Granny couldn't have loved each other more," said Ben, beginning to blub.

The Queen opened her arms and **embraced** him.

27

"Oh, Ben! One didn't mean to make you cry," said the Queen, holding Ben tightly.

"They are happy tears!" he spluttered through sobs. "Promise?"

"I promise!" Ben tried to wipe away the tears with his sleeve, but it was impossible with his cardboard iceberg outfit.

"Here, let one," said the Queen. She reached up her sleeve and pulled out a used tissue.

"You have a used tissue tucked up your sleeve!"

"Of course one does. All grannies do. It's the rules."

She dabbed his eyes and took away the tears. Then she couldn't resist spitting on the tissue and wiping the boy's face with it.

"SPUT!"

"Yuck!" moaned Ben.

"Sorry, force of habit. Still do it to one's children. They hate it! Especially if we are all on show on the balcony of Buckingham Palace!"

Ben chuckled at the thought, before saying, "But, Your Majesty, you never answered my question. Why are you here tonight in the Tower of London stealing your own *Crown Jewels*? It doesn't make any sense!"

The old lady smiled. "Do you have any idea what it's like being the Queen?"

"Not a clue!"

"A lot of smiling and waving and shaking hands and cutting ribbons and hosting balls and being put on show in the back of a giant pram."

"A giant pram?" exclaimed Ben.

"One means a carriage. Like those you see us in at the racecourse at Royal Ascot. It makes us look like posh babies!"

"Oh yes!" replied Ben.

"A lot of all that, and very little excitement!"

Ben scratched his head, before asking, "So is that why you have become the new **BLACK CAT**?"

"Well, yes. A bit of a career change, one knows. Queen to thief. But one has had a long lifetime of being royal. One needed to break out. Do something **bananas!**"

"But this?" spluttered Ben. "What if you get caught?"

"That is part of the thrill!"

"The world would end if people found out the Queen was an international jewel thief!"

"Hardly!" snorted the Queen.

"I suppose you could always pardon yourself."

"Oh yes. One hadn't thought of that. Jolly clever! Just as your grandmother inspired one to become an international jewel thief, she inspired one to put it back too."

"Thank goodness for that," replied Ben.

"That is frightfully important. One hardly needs to

tell you that stealing is wrong."

"But fun?" asked Ben cheekily.

"Well, yes. Fun but wrong. Very wrong if one doesn't put what one stole back. Which is precisely what one had always planned to do. But there's a problem."

"Just the one?" said Ben with a grin.

"Since the heists, the British Museum and Wembley Stadium have upped their security. And one needs to move fast before the police look too closely at those SCRABBLE pieces!"

"Let me help you," said Ben.

"Why would you do that?"

"Because it will be fun. And I thought you'd be all posh and hoity-toity because you are the Queen. But you're not."

"Thank goodness for that!"

"I like you," said Ben with a smile.

"And one really likes you too," she replied before stopping to look at the boy with suspicion. "You're not angling for a knighthood, are you?"

"Nah. Sir Ben Herbert sounds silly! I just want to say thanks for being so nice to me and my grandmother."

"One granny to another! Both **gangstas** at heart."

"Whoever thought that the Queen was a **Gangsta Granny?**"

Just then they heard a jangle of keys outside the door to the Jewel House.

JINGLE! JANGLE!

Then a key in the lock, turning.

CLICK!

And the door opening.

CREAK!

"Beefeaters!" hissed the Queen. "No one must see one here!"

"Well then, we'd better escape."

He took the Queen by the hand, and they tiptoed up the steps. As the Beefeaters shone their lanterns on the *Crown Jewels* to see what had been going on in the Jewel House, the pair slipped out of the open door and into the courtyard.

At that moment, a deafening alarm sounded.

DRING!

The floodlights burst to life.

The Queen and Ben looked at each other, aghast.

"They must know we've been in there!" said Ben.

"One left the SCRABBLE letters! Silly me!"

"Oh no."

"Do you know a way out?" she asked.

"Have you ever been down a sewer?"

"One can't say one has. But one is always willing to try something new!"

"Then follow me!" said Ben as he pulled her away from the scene of the crime.

28

Now that the alarm had been raised, the Tower of London was swarming with Beefeaters!

The old soldiers armed with their poles were calling out into the night to each other.

"HALT! WHO GOES THERE?"

"The entrance to the sewers must be somewhere near here!" hissed Ben.

"But where?" replied the Queen, sounding in a fright.

Ben looked down at her feet. She was standing right on top of a drain cover.

"You are a genius!" he exclaimed.

"Is one?"

"Look down!"

"Oh! So one is!"

The pair sank to their knees and began prising the weighty metal disc up with their fingertips. Just as they heard police sirens and the screech of car tyres…

WOOH! WOOH! WOOH! WOOH!

SCREEEEEEEEEECH!

…Ben spluttered, "After you, ma'am!"

The Queen looked down into the dirty, dark hole. "No! No! After you!"

The boy leaped down, then offered up a helping hand to the Queen. Together they slid the drain cover back into place just as they heard someone running over it.

CLOMP! CLOMP! CLOMP!

Now they were in the old sewage pipe that led out from the Tower of London into the River Thames.

"I hope you can swim, Your Majesty!" said Ben, his voice echoing in the stone pipe.

"It's been a while since one was awarded one's fifty-metre badge, but one will give it one's best shot!"

There were all sorts of nasties down there:

Slime   Muck   Gloop   Rats

Grot   Gunk   Sludge

Goo

And worst of all... *thousand-year-old poo!*

"One can appreciate why they don't include the sewer in the tour of the Tower," remarked the Queen.

"Hold your nose, ma'am!"

"What fun!" said the Queen, pinching her nose and sounding rather **silly**.

Soon the pair were ankle-deep in brown water.

Then knee-deep.

Then waist-deep.

Then chest-deep.

Then neck-deep.

The pair had reached the end of the sewer. Beyond it was the River Thames.

"Close your eyes and hold your breath!" urged Ben.

"Jolly hockey sticks!"

Holding the Queen's hand tightly, he plunged into the cold water.

Together they swam underwater until they finally reached the surface of the river.

"AHHH!"

"URGH!"

They both gasped for air as their heads bobbed up and down.

"We made it!" exclaimed Ben.

"And one has never felt more alive!" yelled the Queen.

It was now late at night and the River Thames was free of boats. Except one. A police launch was speeding straight towards them.

ROAR! went the engine.

The boat bounced up and down on the waves as its siren wailed.

BUMF! BUMF! BUMF!

WOOH! WOOH! WOOH! WOOH!

It was going so fast that there was no way Ben and the Queen could escape.

"We're done for!" he cried.

"Let's hide underwater!" suggested the Queen.

"The boat might run us over!"

"You're right! We are done for! Unless…"

"Unless what!"

"Well, one will hide behind you, and you keep your head down."

"So?"

"They may think you are just some old rubbish floating in the water!"

"They might!"

Actually, it turned out even better than that. When the police launch was almost upon them, one of the officers shouted, "ICEBERG!"

The police on board all screamed.

"ARGH!"

"NOOOO!"

"REMEMBER THE *TITANIC*!"

"SENIOR OFFICERS FIRST!"

"THERE'S NO LIFEBOAT!"

The launch did a dramatic swerve away from the "iceberg" and sped off the way it had come.

"That was lucky!" remarked the Queen.

"I knew this stupid outfit my mum made would come in useful for something," said Ben.

Together they swam across the Thames and managed

to haul themselves out on the other side. Without a word, they looked back at the Tower of London. The castle was now humming with activity. A police helicopter with a searchlight was whirring overhead.

WHIRR!

More and more police cars were arriving at the scene, sirens blazing.

WOOH! WOOH! WOOH! WOOH!

"Where next?" asked Ben.

"One needs to return to Buckingham Palace," replied the Queen.

"Why?"

"That is where Tutankhamun's mask and the **WORLD CUP** are hidden."

"Where?"

"Under one's bed."

"I never hide things under my bed!" said Ben. "That would be the first place my mum and dad would look!"

"Well, one is the Queen, remember? No one looks

under one's bed without permission."

"Makes sense. But Buckingham Palace is on the other side of London! How are we going to get there?"

"Do you have any money on you?" enquired the Queen.

"Nope. I didn't come out with any."

"One neither. But, then again, one is the Queen! One never does!"

"Even though you are on it!"

"Precisely because one is on it."

"Have you got a bus pass?"

"No," replied the Queen. "Although one is old enough for a free one. One has always longed to ride on a bus. Is it as delightful as it looks?"

"No. It's not delightful at all. It's a bus!"

"Oh. So one hasn't missed much?"

"Nothing at all! Let's start walking."

"Jolly good! The sooner we start, the sooner we get there!" agreed the Queen.

However, just as they set off, a police car pulled up right in front of them.

WOOH! WOOH! WOOH! WOOH!

SCREECH!

"Fiddlesticks!" said the Queen.

29

THE RETURN
OF
FUDGE

As if things couldn't get any worse, who should step out of the car but none other than the unmistakable round figure of PC Fudge!

"Well, well, well, what have we here, then?" he said as he trundled over to the pair.

Ben tried to keep his head down so the policeman wouldn't recognise him. Meanwhile, the Queen installed herself behind Ben's soaking-wet cardboard costume that had all but fallen apart. The pair looked guilty, which made Fudge even more suspicious.

"Well, I never! Benjamin Herbert! We meet again!"

"Oh! Hello, PC Fudge," replied the boy. "How super to see you again," he lied.

"Just wait until your mother hears about this! Out late at night. You were meant to be grounded!"

"I was! But then I agreed to be her **ballroom-dance** partner at the Royal Albert Hall."

"Yes. And I have been hearing all about that on my police radio tonight," said Fudge, with a deeply disapproving look at the boy.

"Am I in trouble?" asked Ben.

"The deepest doo-doo that has ever been dooed!"

"Oops," said Ben.

"Oops indeed. And who is this with you?"

"Just an old cockney wench from good ol' London town! Please pay one no heed," replied the Queen, trying her best not to sound like, well… the Queen!

"I know that voice from somewhere!" exclaimed Fudge. The policeman pushed the boy aside to get a better look at the lady. *"Your Majesty!"* he said, dropping to his knees at her feet.

"Oh, please don't grovel!" she snapped. "One can't abide grovellers!"

Fudge tried his best to get up, but couldn't. His legs weren't what they used to be.

"Would you mind awfully?" he begged.

Ben and the Queen then hoisted Fudge to his feet.

"That's better!" he muttered. "Now, Your Majesty, is this boy bothering you? I would gladly arrest him and throw him in prison forever!"

"No! No! No need for that! Actually, this young gentleman saved one from drowning!"

"I did?" asked Ben.

"Yes! You did!"

"I did!" agreed Ben.

"Oh! I can see you are soaking wet!" said Fudge. "Here! Have my jacket!"

With that, he whipped it off and draped it softly over the Queen's shoulders.

"Charmed!" she remarked.

"But how did this boy save you?" asked Fudge.

"Yes, how did I save you?" asked Ben.

The Queen looked a little flustered. "Well, one, er, fell into the river."

"You fell into the river, ma'am?" exploded Fudge. He couldn't believe his ears.

"It's ma'am as in 'ham' not ma'am as in 'farm'," said Ben.

"You fell into the river, ham? I mean, ma'am!"

"Yes!" replied the Queen. "One was coming home from seeing the **ballroom-dancing** competition at the Royal Albert Hall, and one asked one's chauffeur to stop off for a, erm…"

"**Kebab?**" suggested Ben.

"Yes, well remembered," agreed the Queen.

"A **kebab?**" asked Fudge, so surprised he looked as if he might keel over.

"Yes! A **kebab!**" she replied. "And one wanted to sit by the river and enjoy said **kebab.**"

"The chauffeur wouldn't let her eat it in the Rolls-Royce," added Ben.

"Exactly!"

"My mum and dad are exactly the same with me!"

"Mine too!" said Fudge sorrowfully.

"So, one went for a stroll by the river, tripped and fell in. **Splosh!** This boy, by good fortune dressed as an iceberg, leaped in and saved one!"

Fudge took all this in. "What happened to the **kebab?**"

"I tried my best," began Ben, "but I am afraid it drowned."

"Burial at sea," agreed the Queen, doing a mock salute for the drowned **kebab.**

"That's so sad," muttered a distressed-looking Fudge. "I will make sure the police investigation into this brave young man's actions at the Albert Hall earlier tonight is dropped."

"Thank you, PC Fudge," said Ben.

"And, Your Majesty, please let me buy you another **kebab!** It would be an honour!"

"You are too kind!" said the Queen.

"I insist, Your Majesty! To tell the truth, I am feeling a little peckish myself. I could murder a **kebab!**"

"And me," said Ben.

"Well then, let's stop chattering and get going!" announced the Queen. "To the **kebab** shop! And don't spare the horses!"

30

It was thrilling racing through London at night in the back of a police car. Fudge even put the siren and the flashing blue lights on as a treat.

WOOH! WOOH! WOOH! WOOH!

Buying a late-night **kebab** didn't count as an emergency, however hungry they were, but Fudge had

Her Majesty the Queen in the back seat, so he was showing off.

"I got you a doner **kebab** with chilli sauce, Your Majesty," announced Fudge as he sat in the front seat and passed the bag of food back. Immediately, the mouth-watering aroma of fast food filled the car.

"Thank you, my good man," said the Queen. "I think you have forgotten the silverware."

"The what?" asked the policeman.

"And the bone china!"

"You don't eat doner **kebabs** on a plate with a knife and fork, Your Majesty," said Ben as he unwrapped his.

"No? Then how on earth is said doner **kebab** consumed?"

"With your hands!"

"What fun!" cooed the Queen, and she took a big bite, squirting chilli sauce all over Fudge's face.

CHOMP!

SPLURGE!

Ben burst out laughing. "HA! HA! HA!"

"Oops!" she said. "I think you have a tiny bit of chilli sauce on your face."

"Don't worry, Your Majesty, I will eat it later!" replied Fudge. "I think it fortunate that you stayed in the vehicle, by the way. The **kebab**-shop owner had a photograph of you on the wall."

"How wonderful. One must remember the place," she said, straining to read the sign. "ABRA KEBABRA! That's easy to remember. One will telephone ABRA KEBABRA to see if they can do the catering for the next royal wedding!"

"Where to now, Your Majesty?" asked Fudge, licking the chilli sauce off his face.

"One can't return to Buckingham Palace looking like this!" she said, indicating her wet *BLACK CAT* suit, which now had bits of lamb, tomato, lettuce, cabbage, onion, cucumber and, of course, chilli sauce all down it! "Whatever would one's butler say?"

"So where are we going?" asked Ben.

"Might one go back to your family home so one could change one's clothes?" she asked.

"No! No! No!" he replied. "My mum and dad will be furious with me for mucking up the dance routine."

"I am sure they must be worried about you," she replied.

"You don't know my mum and dad. All they worry about is **ballroom dancing**."

"Very well. Where else, then?" mused the Queen.

"My mum won't let me have people back any more," said Fudge. "I had a party and we ate everything in the fridge."

"How many people were there?" she asked.

"Just me and PC Cake."

"Oh."

"She likes her food and all. Even took a bite out of the fridge."

"I know someone who can help us!" said Ben.

"Who?" asked Fudge.

"Yes, whom do you know?" asked the Queen.

Ben smiled. "Ma'am, do you know a shop called Raj's News?"

31

RAJ MEETS THE QUEEN

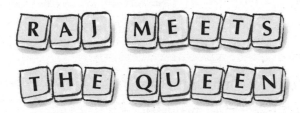

VROOM!

WOOH! WOOH! WOOH! WOOH!

Ben, PC Fudge and the Queen set off across London to Raj's shop at terrific speed.

The wonderful thing about riding in a police car with the lights flashing and the siren blaring is that all the other vehicles on the road get out of your way and you...

don't have to stop at traffic lights…

can take a shortcut across a park if you want to…

are allowed to go the wrong way on one-way
    streets…

can overtake absolutely everyone…

can zoom round tight corners…

can drive on the wrong side of the road…

don't have to slow down in built-up areas…

can't get done for speeding…

and you look DEAD COOL!

Ben and the Queen had barely finished their **kebabs** by the time Fudge brought the police car to a screeching halt outside Raj's shop.

SCREECH!

Now there were bits of **kebab** all over the floor, the seats, the ceiling, the windows and everyone inside.

What's more, the pair in the back had gone a putrid shade of green. Scoffing food on what was wilder than the wildest roller-coaster ride was enough to make you want to vomit. They all but fell out of the back of the police car when Fudge opened the door. They had to hold each other up to make their way to the shop front.

"I will wait by the car, ma'am," said Fudge. "See if I can hoover up any of this **kebab** mess – with my mouth."

It was now the dead of night, and Ben was sure Raj would be tucked up in bed. So he called to the window of the flat above the shop.

"Raj! RAJ!"

But there was no answer.

"RAJ! RAJ! WAKE UP!"

While this was happening, the Queen found a stone on the ground.

"This should do the trick," she said, and she hurled the stone at the window.

SMASH!

"Oops!" said the Queen.

Immediately, Raj, dressed in stripy pyjamas, appeared at the broken window.

"Who threw that?" he demanded, suddenly sounding very much like a headteacher. "Ben? Was that you?"

"No."

"Then who threw it?"

There was silence for a moment.

"I said, 'Who threw that?'"

Eventually, the Queen piped up, "One did!"

"Oh! One did, did one?"

The Queen nodded her head.

"Who do you think you are?" snapped Raj, looking down on the pair.

"Raj, this is *Her Majesty the Queen!*" replied Ben.

"Of course she is! And I'm Willy Wonka!" called Raj. "Wait right there!"

In moments, the metal shutters were wound up, and Raj bustled the pair inside.

"I don't want you waking up all the neighbours!" he said.

"One offers one's sincerest condolences for your smashed window," announced the Queen.

"Now, who are you?" demanded Raj.

"One is *Her Majesty the Queen!*" she replied haughtily.

"This is some sort of prank! You are some bloke off the telly in disguise! Let me pull that false nose of yours off!" exclaimed Raj.

"Unhand one, sir!" cried the Queen as Raj tugged on her nose.

"RAJ! STOP!" pleaded Ben, pulling his friend away. "I know it's crazy, but this really is the Queen!"

Raj realised his mistake, and terror blazed in his

eyes. "I beg your pardon, *Your Most Royal Majestical Highness.*" He fell to his knees. "Please don't lock me up in the Tower for **treason!**"

"Oh! One hasn't done that for years!" said the Queen, her lips pursed. "Although one still could. Now, up we get, please!"

"A cheeky **knighthood** while I'm down here, then?" asked Raj, reaching for a Curly Wurly and handing it to her to use as a sword.

"Up we get!" she pressed.

He took a good look at her. "Seeing your face reminds me that I must buy a stamp!"

The Queen sighed wearily and looked at Ben, who shrugged.

"May I interest *Your Majestical Majesty* in one of my special offers?" continued Raj. "Seventeen sherbet Dib Dabs for the price of sixteen? I will throw in free an only slightly chewed fruit pastille!"

"This man is off his rocker!" was the Queen's verdict.

"That's why everyone loves him," said Ben. "Now,

Raj, the Queen needs your help."

Raj saluted. "Raj of the World-Famous Raj's News at your service, ma'am!"

32

TOP-SECRET MISSION

At once, Raj set about finding some dry clothes for Ben and the Queen. However, all he had were his unsold costumes from Halloween.

"This is your size, Your Majesty," said Raj, handing her a lobster costume.

"One has never dressed as a lobster before. What fun!" she said, taking the costume behind the card carousel to change.

Next, Raj picked up one of his princess outfits. Before he could say a thing, Ben snapped, "NO!"

"What do you mean, no?" asked Raj.

"No means no! I am never, ever, ever dressing up as a princess!"

"But you would look so pretty!" Raj implored.

"NO!"

"Well, the lobster outfits are too big for you."

The Queen reappeared with hers on.

"Red is so your colour!" remarked Raj.

"Oh, why thank you, Mr Raj. Now come on, Ben. You can't stay in those wet things – you will catch your death of cold!"

"But—"

"No buts, Benjamin! Put it on! That's an order from your Queen!"

Ben harumphed and disappeared behind the card carousel. Moments later, he reappeared awkwardly. He was dressed as a princess with the grumpiest look on his face.

"You know I said how pretty you would look as a princess?" began Raj.

"Yep."

"I was wrong."

Then, with the Queen's blessing, Ben told Raj the whole story. They made him swear to keep it secret, which he did, with one hand on his heart and another on a copy of *The Beano*.

Now they needed his help to put the **WORLD CUP** and the mask of Tutankhamun back where they'd been taken from.

"This calls for the *RAJ RACER!*" exclaimed Raj.

"Ooh! Does it go fast?" enquired the Queen.

"No!" replied Ben. "It would be quicker to get the bus." He looked out of the window of the shop to see Fudge licking the car windscreen. "I know!" he exclaimed. "We'll borrow the police car!"

"Fudge would never allow it," replied the Queen. "And he must never know the truth."

"There must be some way of persuading him!" said Ben.

After the Queen had called him into Raj's shop, Fudge was given his orders. "Now," she began, "PC Fudge, as a loyal and faithful servant of the Crown, one needs you to take part in a highly dangerous and **top-secret** mission."

Fudge's eyes lit up with glee. "Ma'am, my middle name is **'danger'**!"

"Is it?" asked Raj.

"No, it's Kimberley."

"Doesn't have quite the same ring to it, does it?" remarked Ben.

"Come now, gentlemen!" said the Queen. "Fudge! One needs you to stay here at Raj's News and guard all the sweeties and chocolate. With your life! Do you understand one?"

The policeman looked around at all the goodies in Raj's shop. This was a treasure trove for someone who loved their treats sweet.

"Loud and clear, ma'am! If I get peckish, am I allowed to help myself to anything?"

"NO!" snapped Raj.

"YES!" she replied. "One is the Queen, so, Mr Raj, you are overruled! Within reason, of course. Don't go bananas!"

"I will exercise restraint, ma'am!" promised Fudge, helping himself to a huge bag of marshmallows.

Raj growled like a dog guarding his bone. "Grrrr!"

"Excellent! Now one just needs your car keys!" said the Queen, holding out her hand expectantly.

"My car keys?" replied the policeman, his mouth full of pink marshmallows.

"Yes. Chop! Chop!"

"I beg your pardon, ma'am, but I am not allowed to give anyone the keys to my police vehicle!"

"Hand them over!"

"I can't!"

"Raj!" said the Queen. "Confiscate that bag of marshmallows."

The newsagent went to swipe them away, but before he could Fudge reached into his trouser pocket and produced a set of car keys.

"Thank you kindly!" said the Queen as she snatched them out of his hand and marched out of the shop.

DING!

The Queen slid into the driving seat as Raj and Ben bundled into the back. She turned the key and revved the engine.

BRUM! BRUM!

Fudge looked on from Raj's shop window, his hand now deep in a jar of toffee bonbons.

"Not my bonbons!" cried Raj.

Ben looked out of the back window. For a moment, he was sure he spotted a pork-pie hat nestling in a bush.

No…

It was late.

Way past Ben's bedtime.

His mind must be playing tricks on him.

"Right. Enough about your bonbons!" announced the Queen. "Let one see what this bad boy can do!"

With that, she stamped her foot down hard on the accelerator pedal.

STOMP!

The police car sped off into the night, and into a whole new adventure.

 *VROOOOM!*

33

SEVEN CORGIS SLEEPING

For an elderly lady, the Queen was an exceedingly fast driver. In no time, the police car had screeched to a halt outside the gates of Buckingham Palace.

SCREECH!

One of the Queen's Guard tapped on the window, and asked, "Please could I see your pass?"

"This is one's pass!" replied the Queen, pointing to her face.

"*Your Majesty!*" he said, bowing. "Forgive me! I didn't recognise you!"

"Forgiven!"

"There was a great deal of concern as to your whereabouts."

"Oh, was there?"

"I will alert the police to call off the search, as you are home safe and sound."

"Please do."

"Yes, we were expecting you back here hours ago."

"There is a simple explanation for that," replied the Queen.

"Oh yes, ma'am?"

"One stopped off for a **kebab!**"

The guard was shocked. "A **k-k-kebab,** ma'am?" he spluttered.

"Yes. A doner **kebab.** It was absolutely scrumdiddlyumptious."

"Very good. And may I ask why you are dressed as a lobster, ma'am?"

"One was trying to go incognito! OPEN THE GATES!"

The gates opened and the car sped into the courtyard.

"Wow! It's cool being the Queen!" remarked Ben.

"It can be. Sometimes," she replied.

"How do I apply?" asked Raj.

The Queen smiled and pulled up outside the main entrance to Buckingham Palace.

It was now the early hours of the morning, and except for the soldiers on guard duty there was no one else about. Just as well, as it would be difficult to explain why the Queen had arrived home from the Royal Albert Hall so late, dressed as a lobster, driving a police car.

"Quick! Let's grab the loot and get out of here!" she hissed.

"Can we have a full guided tour?" asked Raj.

"Not tonight!" snapped the Queen.

She led the pair inside one of the most famous buildings in the world. Three centuries old, the palace had been home to the British royal family since Queen Victoria ascended the throne in 1837. It was magnificent on the inside, just as you might expect it to be.

Oil paintings adorning the walls

Ornamental wallpaper

Velvet curtains

Marble fireplaces

Gold ornaments

Bronze statues

Antique furniture

Leatherbound books

Corgi hair everywhere

Silk carpets

"I thought it would be posh," said Ben, his eyes wide with amazement, "but I never thought it would be this posh. This is posher than posh. This is **poshtastic!**"*

"Thank you kindly!"

"Must take you forever to hoover, though," observed Raj.

"Shush! One doesn't want to wake anyone up!"

The three tiptoed along the long corridors, up the sweeping staircase and into the Queen's bedroom. It was fit for a Queen, which was just as well.

The room looked unchanged for decades. There was a dressing table with an antique leather jewellery box on top. Neatly arranged on shelves were old black-and-white photographs in highly polished silver frames. However, the room was dominated by an elegant wooden four-poster bed, furnished with a cream silk bedcover.

On her bed Ben counted not one, not two, not three, not four, not five, not six, but seven corgis!

They were snoring and trumping away as sleeping dogs do.

---

* A real word you will find in your **Walliamsictionary** that means very, very, very, very, very, very, very, very, very, very posh.

ZZZZ! ZZZZ! **ZZZZ!**

PFFT! PFFT! **PFFT!**

"Don't wake the dogs!" whispered the Queen.

Raj and Ben stayed silent and nodded in agreement.

"They'll bark the palace down!"

The Queen shut and locked her door before pointing under the bed, where she'd hidden both the mask of Tutankhamun and the **WORLD CUP.** This was going to be one tricky manoeuvre: how to get the stolen treasure out from under the bed without waking seven sleeping corgis!

It sounded like a board game or a ride at a theme park.

But it wasn't.

Well, not yet.

The Queen moved slowly as she sank to her knees, gesturing for the other two to follow her lead. Then she lifted the silk bedcover.

Glistening in the dark were two of the most valuable objects in the world. Ben and Raj reached their hands under the bed, and pulled out the **WORLD CUP.** They laid it down gently on the silk rug on the floor.

The Queen smiled and nodded.

Next was the trickier part. The mask of Tutankhamun was much heavier, and it needed all three of them to drag it out from under the bed. Taking it slowly, they just managed to place it on the silk rug without a sound.

Then they stood up and took a breath.

PFFT!

Ben and Raj were startled at the sound. The Queen shook her head. This was nothing to worry about – just another corgi bottom banger. Then her eyes began to water. This was a particularly **STINKODOROUS*** one!

---

* *A real word created by the renowned author David Walliams, collected in his own special made-up dictionary, the* **Walliamsictionary.** *Available at all bad bookshops.*

Ben and Raj looked at each other in horror. This one was DEADLY! They thought they might choke. Or pass out. Or both.

Now there was an urgent need to get these treasures out of the Queen's bedroom as fast as they possibly could.

The Queen lifted the **WORLD CUP** by herself and gestured for Raj and Ben to carry the solid gold mask between them. However, when Raj bent down to pick it up, there was that sound again.

PFFT!

Raj's cheeks went red. The Queen looked at him in disgust. This wasn't a corgi bottom banger! This was a Raj bottom banger!

It was so loud that it woke all seven corgis up at once.

"YAP!" "YAP!" "YAP!" "YAP!" "YAP!" "YAP!" "YAP!"

They barked and barked and barked.

"How come they can sleep through their own bottom whoopsies, but not one of mine!" exclaimed Raj.

"SHUSH! SHUSH! SHUSH!" shushed Ben, trying

his best to calm them all down. But the more he tried the more they barked.

"YAP!" "YAP!" "YAP!" "YAP!" "YAP!" "YAP!" "YAP!"

Now the dogs had sunk their teeth into the bottom of Raj's pyjamas and were yanking away.

CHOMP!

"They are going to wake up the whole of London!" exclaimed the Queen. "One needs to get out of here! And fast!"

Ben and Raj picked up the mask and headed for the door, corgis trailing in their wake.

"YAP!" "YAP!" "YAP!" "YAP!" "YAP!" "YAP!" "YAP!"

Just as they reached it, there was a loud banging from the other side.

THUMP! THUMP! THUMP!

"Excuse me, Your Majesty!" came a posh voice. "It is Butler the butler here. Is everything in order?"

"Yes, thank you, Butler!" called the Queen.

"We were most concerned about you. There was chaos at the Royal Albert Hall and there was great confusion as to your whereabouts."

'Well, one is home now! Thank you!"

"I am relieved, but it is most unlike you to be so late."

"One stopped off for a **kebab!**"

"Very good, ma'am. May I come in, ma'am? I was sure I could hear voices a moment ago!"

"Not this way – we have to find another way out!" hissed the Queen.

"Pardon me, ma'am! I didn't quite catch that!" called Butler.

"Nothing, Butler!"

"Is that his name or his job?" asked Ben.

"Yes, his name is Butler, and his job is butler. It's frightfully easy to remember!"

"YAP!" "YAP!" "YAP!" "YAP!" "YAP!" "YAP!" "YAP!"

"Something isn't right, ma'am!" said Butler the butler. "Forgive me, but I can tell by the tone of your voice. Please open the door at once!"

From the other side, he rattled the door handle and thudded his shoulder against the door.

The Queen looked lost for words, so Raj leaped in, affecting her voice.

"Everything is fine and tickety-boo, Butler the butler the butler!" he called out.

He sounded ridiculous!

Just then another of the corgis took a dislike to this intruder.

"GRRR!"

It launched itself at Raj and bit him on the bum.

CHOMP!

"OWEE!" cried Raj, suddenly going back into his own voice. "MY BOTTOM!"

"SHUSH!" shushed Ben.

But it was no use.

"MY BOTTOM IS BEING EATEN ALIVE!"

"I am off to sound the alarm, ma'am!" cried Butler.

"I will be back with the soldiers in moments!"

His footsteps echoed away down the corridor outside.

"Let's make a run for it!" hissed the Queen.

She unlocked her bedroom door, and the three rushed out, carrying the treasure, with the seven corgis pursuing them all the way.

"YAP!" "YAP!" "YAP!" "YAP!"
"YAP!" "YAP!" "YAP!"

"Shush!" shushed the Queen, but to no avail. They

just kept yapping at the two strangers, and who can blame them? They did look like robbers making off with stolen loot. The problem was that the dogs were so noisy. They were going to alert the soldiers as to exactly where the three were in the palace.

Up ahead, perched on a chandelier, was a **black** 🐾**cat**.

Could it be THE **black** 🐾**cat**?

"Ma'am, do you have a cat?" asked Ben.

"No! Of course one does not have a cat. One's dogs would chase it day and night."

"Then whose cat is that, swinging from the chandelier?"

"How did it get in here?" cried the Queen.

As they approached, the cat miaowed loudly at the dogs to get their attention.

This stopped the seven dogs in their tracks, and instantly they fell silent. A cat was so much better to chomp on than someone's pyjama bottoms.

Then – "YAP!" "YAP!" "YAP!" "YAP!" "YAP!" "YAP!" "YAP!" – they barked again,

even louder than before.

The cat dangled down from the chandelier by its tail, then let out the fiercest hiss: "HISS!"

The corgis all whimpered: "HHHMMM!" Then they scrambled away with their tails between their legs. Literally.

"Thank you!" called Ben to the cat.

"One is not convinced the cat can understand you," remarked the Queen.

"Oh, I think she can!" he replied.

The Queen looked confused, but Ben wasn't sharing his secret with her. The **black cat** had protected him so many times since Granny had gone, just like Granny had in life. Perhaps the spirit of Granny was with the cat somehow?

YOU ARE ONLY OLD ONCE!

Soon the three adventurers were back at Fudge's police car, and jumped in just as the elderly butler and the Queen's Guard caught up with them.

VROOM!

The Queen stamped her foot on the accelerator pedal, but not before the brave butler leaped on to the bonnet of the police car.

THUNK!

"MA'AM! STOP THE CAR!" he cried as they sped off through the courtyard.

The old man's face was pressed up against the windscreen. The Queen flicked on the windscreen wipers in the hope of repelling him.

Sweep! Swoop! Sweep! Swoop!

But the butler was not letting go.

"Don't worry, Butler! One is just off for a joyride in a stolen police car! One will be back in time for breakfast!"

When she was far enough away from the guards who were running after them, she brought the car to a slow stop.

"You are a wonderful butler, Butler," said the Queen, "but please don't worry about one! One is having the time of one's life!"

The butler slid off the bonnet and paced over to the driver's window.

"Enjoy your freedom, ma'am. Goodness knows you've earned it!"

"Most kind, Butler."

"Egg and soldiers in the morning, ma'am?"

"You know one well."

"And may I say you look radiant as a lobster. But who, pray, is this dear little girl?"

Ben harumphed. "HMMM!"

Just then the Queen's Guard caught up with the police car. Those ahead were closing the gates.

"One would love to stop and chat, but one has some mayhem to cause! Farewell!" called the Queen.

The butler gave the Queen a proud little salute before she raced off in the police car.

VROOM!

"We won't get through the gates!" exclaimed Ben. They were closing fast and the car was too wide to pass through them.

"Everyone lean over to my side!"

Ben and Raj did as they were told, and the car tipped over on to two wheels.

"You're not going to—" began Raj.

"Oh yes one is! One is only old once!" cried the Queen as she made the car speed up.

VROOM!

"I can't look!" cried Raj, cowering behind the mask.

The car just managed to pass through the gates. Raj

and Ben then swung over to the other side of the car, and it fell back on to four wheels.

"You are BANANAS, Your Majesty!" said Ben.

"Most kind!" she replied, and they sped off into the night.

35

The first stop was Wembley Stadium to return the **WORLD CUP.** As the car screeched to a halt outside, Ben asked, "How did you break in last time?"

"One flew in and landed on the pitch with one's very own handbag hang-glider."

"Very la-de-da!" remarked Raj.

"Where on earth does one get a handbag hang-glider?" asked Ben. "I'd like one!"

"On a visit to the headquarters of one's Secret Service, of course!"

"Oh, of course!" replied Ben cheekily. "Why didn't I guess?"

"Where is the handbag hang-glider now?" asked Raj.

"On the top of the Tower of London where I left it," said the Queen.

"Oh!" said Raj.

"Yes... oh," she replied.

"I know a way!" announced Ben proudly.

"Is this a clue you came across in **PLUMBING WEEKLY?**" enquired the Queen.

"Not quite," he replied. "From some books I took out of the library. The grass pitch has a new high-tech sprinkler system..."

"One guessed it might be something plumbing-related!"

"...so there must be a large pipe leading from the water tank right into the stadium. If we can find the tank, then we should be able to find a way in. But it will be a tight squeeze!"

Raj popped his hand in the air.

"Yes, Raj," said Ben.

"When you say 'we', who do you mean?"

"I mean us three. Although someone will have to stay at the water tank to open and close the valve."

"Bagsy that!" said Raj.

The Queen set off on a slow lap round the stadium, but Ben shouted, **"STOP!"**

He'd spotted a sign on a large metal box that read: **WATER SHUT-OFF CONTROL VALVE.**

"It must be under there!"

They lifted the metal cover in no time to reveal a water tank as big as a swimming pool.

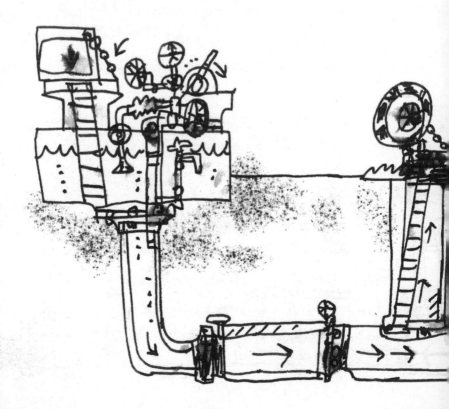

"I think it's best I go alone, Your Majesty," began Ben. "When the valve opens, water is going to rush down that tube. We'll be sloshing around inside like it's a water slide!"

"One has always wanted to go on a water slide!" replied the Queen.

"Well, let's go, then. Raj, when I say so, spin this valve to open the tube."

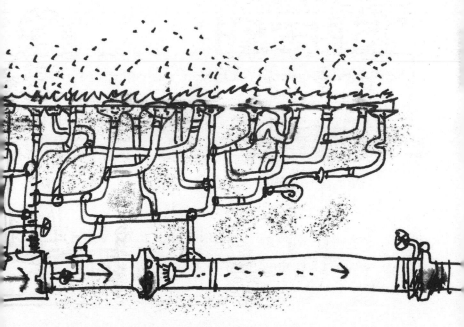

"Right-ho!" he replied.

"Ladies first!" said Ben.

Still clutching the gold **WORLD CUP** statue, the Queen leaped down the manhole into the water tank below.

SPLOSH!

"Is it cold?" called Ben.

"I DON'T WANT TO S-S-S-SPOIL THE S-S-S-SURPRISE!" replied the Queen, her teeth chattering.

Ben winced and jumped.

SPLOSH!

The shock of the cold water was enough to make him gasp.

"AAAHHH!"

Then he called up his instructions to Raj.

"Pull the top lever all the way to the right... NOW!"

Raj did as he was told. "Done!"

Instantly, the pair in the water tank could feel themselves swirling downwards, as if someone had pulled the plug in a giant bath. They were sucked through a narrow pipe. Just as Ben had warned, it was exactly like a water slide.

"WHEE!"

cried the Queen, speeding down the pipe.

"KEEP HOLD OF THE WORLD CUP!" called Ben, his voice echoing in the long metal tube.

Soon they found themselves completely underwater as the pressure built up to feed the sprinklers under the pitch. Ben grabbed hold of a ladder with one hand, and the Queen with the other. The ladder led up a tube to a hatch on top, just as you might see on a submarine.

Ben spun the lock on the hatch and opened it on to the Wembley Stadium football pitch. He climbed out and then helped the Queen manage the last few steps. They stood together in silence for a moment, watching the pitch being sprayed with water in the moonlight. It was **eerie** and beautiful in equal measure. There was *magic* in the air.

"Don't ever forget this moment," said the Queen.

"I won't," replied Ben, shivering at the cold.

"This is a special memory. It belongs to us. And us only. Nobody can take it away from us."

They stood in silence for a moment. Then the Queen continued, "Cold, isn't it?"

"Absolutely **FREEZING.**"

"Let's put this thing back in the exhibition and get out of here!"

"Which way?"

"Through those doors there, if memory serves one

correctly," replied the Queen, pointing to some tall metal double doors behind the goal. "But it looks like they have reinforced them. They were glass last time."

"They look impossible to get through!"

"We will think of something. Now let's go!"

However, no sooner had they taken a step, than the floodlights lit up the pitch.

FLUNK!

WHIRR!

For a moment, Ben was blinded by the brightness. All he could see in front of his face was a wall of white.

Then he heard an engine starting.

BRRRUUUMMM!

Not a car engine. A lawnmower engine. It was only when Ben could see again that he realised the true horror. Someone was sitting on top of a colossal lawnmower. It was less a lawnmower, more a **tank.** Whatever it was, it was heading straight for them!

Ben and the Queen shared a look of PURE DREAD!

Any moment now, they were going to be face to face with those giant revolving blades!

BBBRRRUUUMMM!!!

36

TRESPASSERS

"WHO ARE YOU?" demanded the Queen as the giant lawnmower drew closer and closer and closer.

BRRRUUUMMM!

Ben spotted that the lawnmower had a sign on its side that read: **THE BEAST.** He wasn't sure if that was referring to the man or the machine.

"I AM THE GROUNDSMAN! AND YOU ARE TRESPASSING ON MY GRASS!" the man shouted back. He was a short, stubby fellow with a bald head. He could be mistaken for a giant's thumb. "DO YOU KNOW WHAT

HAPPENS TO TRESPASSERS WHO DARE STEP ON MY GRASS?"

"NO!" replied Ben over the noise of the engine. "BUT I HAVE A FEELING YOU ARE GOING TO TELL US!"

"THEY GET MOWED!"

"This man is absolutely crackers!" cried the Queen. "Let's make a run for it!"

But, whichever way they ran, the groundsman chased after them.

BBBRRRUUUMMM!!!

"I've got an idea!" hissed Ben as they ran in and out of the fountains of water spraying the pitch. "Why don't we lead him towards the metal doors? We might be able to kill two birds with one stone!"

"Clever boy!"

So the pair dashed towards the doors, the Beast trailing in their wake. The fountains of water were spraying in the groundsman's face, making it difficult for him to see clearly.

When Ben and the Queen reached the doors, they

turned round to face the groundsman.

"PREPARE TO BE MOWED!" he
cried out, wiping water from his eyes.

"NOW!" shouted Ben.

He and the Queen leaped out of the way just in
time as the Beast ploughed into the tall metal doors.

KRUNK!

The force of the impact threw the groundsman
from his seat.

WHIZZ!

"ARGH!"

He landed in the back
of the net of the goal.

"I WILL GET
YOU!" he shouted, but
he was all tangled up like a fly in a spider's web.

"Not any time soon, by the looks of it," replied the
Queen tartly.

The pair dashed inside the building and stumbled
into the exhibition of football history.

It was a football fan's dream. There were:

The shirts of superstar players

Team flags

Photographs from historic matches

Souvenir programmes

Medals

Trophies

Signed balls

Football boots through the ages

Even a giant mascot or two

Old sticker albums

"Ma'am, are you a football fan?" asked Ben.

"One is not!"

"Me neither! This is completely wasted on us, then!"

"Now, where on earth is the plinth?"

"Plinth Charles?" asked Ben.

"One said 'plinth' not 'prince'!"

There was an empty white stand in the centre of the room.

"Over there!" said Ben.

The Queen looked at the **WORLD CUP** trophy for the last time. "It was fun while it lasted," she said as she kissed it and placed it on the plinth.

But as soon as she did there was the deafening sound of an alarm.

UUUWWUUUWWUUUWWUUU!

"The plinth!" shouted the Queen. "One forgot! It's alarmed!"

"We need to get out of here! And fast!" urged Ben.

Down the corridor they could see the silhouettes

of what looked like a dozen security guards heading straight for them.

STOMP!

STOMP!

STOMP!

went their boots on

the shiny floor.

37

Ben and the Queen raced in the opposite direction, back towards the football pitch. However, waiting there for them was another group of a dozen security guards.

"FOR GOODNESS' SAKE, GET OFF MY GRASS!" shouted the groundsman at them. He was still tangled up in the goal net.

The guards ignored him. They seemed infinitely more interested in catching these two thieves than worrying about some turf.

"We can't go back the way we came in!" said Ben.

The Queen eyed the Beast up and down as if it were a thoroughbred horse. "Do you fancy a ride?" she asked.

"It's our only hope!"

"Hop on!"

The pair clambered up on to the Beast. The Queen struggled with the controls, so Ben turned it on for her.

BBBRRRUUUMMM!

"Why, thank you, kind sir!"

She then spun the steering wheel.

WHIRR!

The giant lawnmower began revolving.

CHUGA-CHUGA-CHUGA!

Immediately, the security guards backed off. None of them wanted to be turned into mincemeat. Now with a clear run, Ben pointed to what looked like a way out.

"THAT WAY, MA'AM!" he shouted over the noise of the engine.

"MY BEAST! GIVE ME BACK MY BEAST!" wailed the groundsman from the net.

"NEVER!" shouted the Queen, clearly enjoying herself a little too much. She steered a course to where Ben was pointing.

The Beast bashed through a set of doors.

BAM!

And another!

BAAM!

And yet another!

BAAAM!

Until it was out of the stadium.

The security guards ran after them.

STOMP!

STOMP!

STOMP!

Circling the building, they saw Raj waiting by the police car. Seeing guards coming from all directions now, he decided to build his part somewhat and quickly put on Fudge's police hat.

"Think you can steal a giant lawnmower, do you? Well, you two are UNDER ARREST! GET IN MY POLICE CAR THAT ONLY SLIGHTLY SMELLS OF KEBAB! NOW!"

Playing their roles, Ben and the Queen slid down from the seat of the Beast. They bowed their heads and said, "Sorry, PC Raj!"

"SORRY ISN'T GOOD ENOUGH!" thundered PC Raj. "I AM TAKING YOU STRAIGHT TO PRISON! WHERE YOU WILL SPEND THE REST OF YOUR LIVES!"

As they slid into the back seat of the police car, Raj turned to the security guards. "Thank you so much. PC Raj will take over from here!"

"If you are a police officer, why are you dressed in your pyjamas?" asked one plucky security guard.

The other security guards all murmured in agreement.

"I'm so deep undercover I'm actually mostly in bed!" Raj replied, before leaping into the driving seat and racing off.

VROOOM!

38

Ben, Raj and the Queen laughed at their escapades.

"HA! HA! HA! We did it!"

They had indeed. Their mission to return the **WORLD CUP** to Wembley Stadium had been a stonking success. Now all they had to do was put the mask of Tutankhamun back in its place at the British Museum and the Queen would be in the clear.

Raj adored being at the wheel of the police car. He put the siren and the flashing lights on to add to the drama.

"PC Raj on the case!" he cried.

"I want this night to go on forever!" said Ben in the back seat.

"One too!" replied the Queen. "But it will last forever in our hearts."

In no time, the police car came to a halt outside the entrance to the British Museum.

The huge columns at the front of the building made it look as if they were in Ancient Greece. The museum had only been founded around three hundred years ago, although it had changed a lot over the next few centuries. It was home to lots and lots of ancient art and antiquities, so it was the perfect place to put the mask of Tutankhamun on display. Well, it *was* until Her Majesty the Queen decided to become the new **Gangsta Granny** and steal it!

The unlikely trio waited until the security guards had passed in front of the entrance before stepping out of the police car. The Queen led the way, with Ben and Raj trailing behind, carrying the mask.

"So how are we going to get into this old place?" asked Raj, huffing and puffing. "This thing weighs more than a box of toffee!"

"Last time one came through one of the underground

tunnels built during the Blitz—" began the Queen, but Ben jumped in.

"That leads all the way from Buckingham Palace!"

"How did you know that?"

"I studied some books in the library about the museum. That was a big clue! The tunnel from your house. I should have known it was you all along!"

"But who would ever suspect Her Majesty the Queen?" she said, rather smugly.

"I will now!" said Raj. "Even if one penny chew goes missing from my shop, I shall blame it on you, ma'am!"

The Queen was rather tickled by this. "Ha! Ha!"

"I need to put this thing down!" complained Raj.

"Me too!" said Ben. "How on earth did you lift it on your own, ma'am?"

"I let my corgis pull it along on a sled! Arctic-style!"

"Proper **gangsta!**" said Ben.

"Please can someone tell me how we are going to get in?" demanded Raj.

"One doesn't know! We would have to go all the

way back to Buckingham Palace to find the entrance to the tunnel!"

"We could just leave the mask here at the front door!" said Raj. "The security guards will have circled round in a moment."

"Someone might steal it!" replied Ben.

The Queen pushed against the front door of the museum, and it opened.

CREAK!

"One's goodness! The door is open!" she exclaimed in astonishment. "Follow one!"

Ben and Raj shared a worried look, before tailing the Queen into the museum.

Inside, it was still and quiet. Too still and too quiet for Ben's liking. The boy felt something was wrong.

"This isn't right," he hissed.

"Maybe someone just left the door unlocked? I sometimes do!" whispered Raj.

"This is the British Museum. People don't just forget to lock the door! It must be a trap!" replied Ben.

"Let's put the mask back and get the blazes out of here!" replied Raj.

Their footsteps echoed around the huge entrance hall. The museum is home to eight million objects. Sadly, our heroes didn't have time to see them all, but they did pass some of the most dazzling artefacts that have survived from ancient civilisations:

THE SUTTON HOO BURIAL SHIP HELMET

This is a bronze helmet from the burial of an Anglo-

 Saxon warrior or king dating back over a thousand years. He was buried in a huge ship along with his treasures. Sutton Hoo is the name of the place in Suffolk where the ship was excavated.

THE LEWIS CHESSMEN

These are chess pieces carved from walrus tusks and whalebone sometime during the twelfth century.

The Fishpool Hoard
Over a thousand gold coins
and pieces of jewellery dating
back to the 1400s. The largest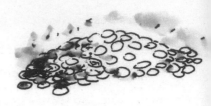
collection of medieval coins ever found in Britain.

Eventually, the three made it to the specially
constructed new exhibition gallery where the mask
of Tutankhamun had been displayed, surrounded by
other treasures from Ancient Egypt. There was:

The Rosetta Stone
This is adorned with hieroglyphs
etched by Ancient Egyptian priests.

The Head of the Pharaoh
This is a gigantic head of Amenhotep III,
a pharaoh who lived more than three
thousand years ago. He wears a double
crown, which tells us he ruled both upper
and lower Egypt.

THE CAT MUMMIES

Aside from human mummies, the museum has cat mummies and even a falcon mummy from Ancient Egypt. People then liked their pets to be buried with them so they would be at their side in the afterlife.

"I don't think I can carry this old thing one step more!" spluttered Raj.

"Me neither!" added Ben.

"Let one help!" said the Queen, lending a hand to carry the solid gold mask for the very last part of its journey. "Ooh! This is heavy!"

"That's what we keep telling you!" moaned Raj.

Just then they heard a familiar sound.

"MIAOW!"

It was the **black cat** again. Only this time it was perched right on top of the pharaoh's head.

"How on earth did that cat get all the way here from Buckingham Palace?" asked the Queen.

"It's not the same cat!" said Raj.

"It is!" replied Ben. He knew. This cat had been around every step of the way, protecting him.

"MIAOW!" it went again. It sounded like it was trying to alert them to something.

It leaped down from the head and tugged at the bottom of Ben's princess costume.

"MIAOW!"

"It's right under my feet!" moaned Raj, and he tried to move it away with his foot.

As he did so, a strange noise came from his back.

TWANG!

"OOF!" he cried in pain. "My back! I can't hold this thing any longer!"

Ben and the Queen took the weight of the mask before sliding it back inside the bulletproof glass case.

"OOF! My back's always playing up! I need to sit down!" said Raj, searching for a seat.

"MIAOW!" warned the cat.

"I'm sorry, Raj! I think the cat is trying to tell us something. We need to get out of here! And fast!" said Ben. "Let me help you!"

"One too!" added the Queen.

The pair took Raj's arms and draped them over their shoulders so they could support his weight. Together, they helped the hobbling hero out of the vast room, slower than a snail, the cat trailing behind.

"NOT SO FAST!" boomed a voice from behind the pharaoh's head.

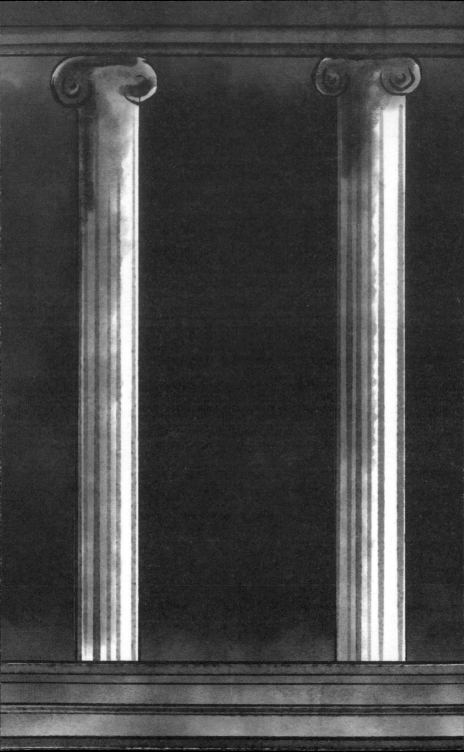

PART FOUR

SHOWDOWN

39

REVENGE OF THE OLDIES!

"W-w-who's there?" demanded Ben, trembling with fear.

A figure stepped out of the shadows into the light. He tipped his pork-pie hat.

That was who the cat had been miaowing about!

"MIAOW!" went the cat again, as if to say, "I told you so." It slunk off like a panther into the darkness of the museum.

"**It is I!** Mr Parker, your friendly neighbourhood **Neighbourhood Watch** group leader, Lower Toddle branch!" said the man. "And you are all under citizen's arrest!"

With that, his army of oldies emerged from their

hiding places and gathered around him.

For once, the Queen looked alarmed.

"Citizen's arrest? Whatever for?" protested Raj. "If it is about selling those pre-sucked sweets in my shop—!"

"It is not about that!" snapped Mr Parker. "But that will be added to the list of crimes! Ben, I knew all along you were an arch-criminal! But why are you dressed as a princess? And why is the lady dressed as a lobster?"

"Never mind about that! How did you get in here?" demanded Ben.

"My sister, Miss Parker, is also a volunteer at the library here at the British Museum. She has a key. We followed you from Raj's shop, which we have had under surveillance for some time!"

"I thought I saw you hiding in the bushes!" exclaimed Ben.

"Mr Parker, you didn't see me dancing around the shop in my undercrackers, did you?" asked a deeply worried Raj.

"A vision that, as much as I might want to, I can never forget. Now, I demand to know, who is your accomplice in the lobster costume?"

"Good evening!" chirped the Queen, keeping her head down. "One is Raj's mother, Mrs Raj!"

"I recognise that voice!" said Miss Parker.

"Me too!" agreed her brother.

"I don't!" said Ben.

"Me neither!" added Raj. "It definitely isn't *Her Majesty the Queen!*"

Ben and the Queen looked at him, aghast that he'd given the game away!

"Oops!" said Raj.

"*Your Majesty!*" exclaimed Mr Parker, taking a step nearer to catch a closer look. "Can it truly be you?"

"Yes!" replied the Queen. "One is one!"

Mr Parker and his fellow do-gooders all instinctively knelt at the feet of their monarch.

"Let's make a run for it!" said Ben.

"No. One is afraid the game is up," said the Queen.

315

"It was all my fault!" exclaimed Ben, eager to protect his new friend. "You should let the Queen walk free!"

The lady looked at the boy, beaming with pride. "No, Ben. It is one who should take all the blame."

"I am happy with that!" agreed Raj.

"I stole the mask of Tutankhamun, the **WORLD CUP** and I would have stolen the *Crown Jewels* if this brave young man hadn't stopped me."

Ben beamed as the Queen stroked his hair.

"But-but-but..." spluttered Mr Parker, "why would Her Majesty the Queen steal her own *Crown Jewels?*"

"Just for the thrill!"

"The *thrill*, ma'am?" asked Miss Parker, utterly perplexed.

"One's entire life has been mapped out for one from birth. Each of our lives can be. I have spent my whole life smiling and waving. I wanted to rebel! Do something bonkers!"

"Ma'am, there is **bonkers** and there is **bonkers**. This is **BONKERTASTIC!**"* remarked Mr Parker.

"That's why it has all been so delicious! But now my adventure is at an end. Arrest me!" she said, holding her wrists out as if to be handcuffed.

"I can't arrest you, *Your Majesty!*" said Mr Parker.

"*I* could!" said a fierce-looking old lady at the back. "Lock her up and throw away the key!"

"Miss Winters! Please!" said Mr Parker. "Sorry about her, ma'am. She gets a little carried away."

"Well then, what are we to do, Mr Parker?" asked the Queen.

"I don't know, ma'am. How would we explain all this?"

"I've got an idea!" said Ben proudly.

"Pray continue," prompted the Queen.

* *Please consult your* **Walliamsictionary** *immediately.*

"Why don't we let Mr Parker and his gang—"

"Group!" corrected Mr Parker. **"Neighbourhood Watch** is a group! You make us sound like a bunch of hooligans!"

"Why don't we let Mr Parker and his group get all the credit for returning the mask of Tutankhamun?"

"Go on!" said Mr Parker, eagerness in his eyes.

"He could say he and his group tracked down the gang of thieves, and in a daring and heroic struggle they got away, but he managed to wrestle this mask, one of the greatest treasures of the world, off them."

"Hmm. I like the sound of that, boy!" agreed Mr Parker. "And then, of course, to say thank you, we are all invited to tea and buns at Buckingham Palace."

"At your earliest convenience!" replied the Queen.

There were murmurs of approval from all the oldies.

"Oh! A nice cup of tea!"

"And a slice of cake!"

"Lemon drizzle for me, dear!"

"I can't have marzipan. It brings me out in a rash!"

"Will there be scones and jam?"

"Not raspberry jam, please! The pips get stuck in my teeth!"

"I can't do Wednesdays. I have me bridge club on Wednesdays."

"Buckingham Palace? I do hope we meet the Queen!"

"Lock her up and throw away the key!"

Well, *nearly* all were murmurs of approval.

"And one would like to add," continued the Queen, "that people like you, Mr Parker, and your gang, I mean, *group*, are the backbone of our great nation. Older people fighting crime, keeping our streets safe. Britain needs more people like you!"

Ben rolled his eyes as Mr Parker welled up.

"And, as such, I would like to award you, Mr Parker, a knighthood!"

"What?" exclaimed Raj. "That's not fair!"

Mr Parker took off his hat, fell to his knees and began blubbing.

"BOO! HOO! HOO! This is the happiest day of my life!" he said through a river of tears.

"It sounds like it!" remarked Raj sarcastically.

"Would someone be so kind as to fetch one a sword?" asked the Queen.

"Don't kill him just yet, ma'am," said Raj.

"No, no, silly! It's to **knight** him!"

"I'll get it!" called Mr Parker, springing to his feet and racing off around the British Museum, looking for one. In an instant, he had returned with what looked like an Ancient Roman sword.

"Ah!" exclaimed the Queen. "The Sword of Tiberius, no less!"

She took the iron sword out of its gilded scabbard and admired it for a moment.

"Was he a friend?" asked Raj.

"For goodness' sake! He died two thousand years ago!" exclaimed the Queen.

Like a faithful pet hoping for a treat, Mr Parker knelt at the Queen's feet. **"Ready!"**

"For services to the **Neighbourhood Watch,** Lower Toddle branch," she began, "I award you the title of **Sir Nosy Parker!**"

Mr Parker was so overjoyed he looked as if he might float away in a giant bubble of happiness.

"Oh! Thank you, thank you, thank you, *Your Majesty!*" he exclaimed, kissing the feet of her lobster costume.

"Please stop grovelling!" she snapped. "One can't abide grovellers!"

Mr Parker then clambered up to his knees and began kissing the Queen's hands.

"Off! You are worse than one of one's corgis!"

"A thousand apologies, *Your Majesty!*"

"Well," began the Queen, "as much as one would love to stand around here in a soaking-wet lobster costume having one's hands and feet kissed by a complete stranger, we do have to go!"

"Of course, *Your Most Royal of Royal Highnessnesses.*"

"You can alert the police as soon as we are gone, and one will see you all at the palace for tea and buns!"

With that, Ben, Raj and the Queen

disappeared.

40

"What are you two in the back sulking about?" asked the Queen from the driving seat.

It was true. Ben and Raj were in the most incredible sulk.

"How could you?" moaned Ben.

"How could one what?"

"Give Mr Parker a **knighthood!** We will never hear the last of it!" added Raj.

It was the end of a long night, and the sun was rising. The frost-dusted streets were bathed in a blazing orange light.

"Dawn!" she exclaimed. "Time we all got to our beds!"

323

"OH!" shouted Ben, suddenly remembering something.

He gave the Queen such a fright that she spun the steering wheel and the police car swerved on to the other side of the road.

SCREECH!

It nearly hit the fleets of police cars that were racing in the opposite direction with their lights flashing and sirens blazing.

VROOM!

WOOH! WOOH! WOOH! WOOH!

They were on their way to the British Museum, no doubt.

"Pardon one?" said the Queen.

"I almost forgot. There is one last clue that links you to the crimes, ma'am!"

"What's that?" she asked.

"Your waxwork!"

"Of course!" she replied. "One forgot too!"

"What waxwork?" asked Raj.

"The one of the Queen in the Albert Hall that was

used as a decoy!" replied Ben.

"Indeed, young man," said the Queen. "We need to return it to Madame Tussauds right away!"

The police car took a sharp turn in the direction of the Royal Albert Hall. With the Queen's race-car driving skills, they were there in no time.

SCREECH!

Ben, Raj and the Queen slipped in through a back entrance, posing as cleaners in brown overcoats they'd found hanging from hooks inside. The hall was being cleaned up after the chaos Ben had caused in the dance competition. There were police cordons up all over the place, including around the royal box. The Queen had the key for the door to the box. Once inside, they were relieved to see that the waxwork was still sitting there exactly where the Queen had put it. They picked it up and carried it back out the way they'd come as fast as they could.

Now in the police car there were two Queens: the real one in the driving seat and the waxwork one in the passenger seat.

Ben and Raj found this most peculiar, as the waxwork was so lifelike it looked more like the Queen than the Queen!

The car skidded to a halt outside Madame Tussauds.

SCREECH!

The waxwork museum was about to open for the day and there was already a long queue of tourists outside. It was now a race against time to put the waxwork back into its place before the museum was teeming with visitors.

"Handle one with care!" snapped the Queen as she watched the pair struggling to drag the waxwork of her out of the police car. The dummy's head banged against the roof of the car.

BOOF!

"Ouch!" cried the real Queen.

"That can't have hurt!" said Ben.

"It wasn't even your head!" added Raj.

"It's the principle! Now, how are we going to get one in without everyone knowing it is one?" she asked, indicating the waxwork.

"We should pretend it's a real person!" suggested Ben.

"I have a brilliant idea!" exclaimed Raj from the feet end of the dummy. He whipped the bottom end of the dress up over the head.

SWISH!

Now you couldn't see the dummy's face. But you could see its Union Jack bloomers!

"Now we don't know it's you! I'm such a clever clog!" said Raj.

"For the last time, Raj! It's *clogs*!" exclaimed Ben.

"No! No! No!" snapped the Queen. "This won't do! You can see one's… Well, one can't even bring oneself to say the word!"

"Knickers?" asked Ben mischievously.

"Undercrackers?" suggested Raj.

"Trollies?"

"Drawers?"

"Bottom warmers?"

The Queen interrupted. "What a rude pair you are! Bottom warmers, indeed! I must remember that phrase to use when I next open Parliament… Let's just call them… unmentionables."

"Well," began Raj, "how do you think we can hide the dummy's face, ma'am?"

"It's not a dummy – it's a waxwork! One doesn't mind how we hide one's face, but it shouldn't be at the expense of showing one's unmentionables. Let's treat one with decorum at all times, please!"

"This is all well and good, but how are we going to get into the museum?" asked Ben.

"Last time I broke in via the Underground system. One has one's own private tube train," replied the Queen.

"Of course you do!" chuckled Ben. "But right now we don't have time for all that malarkey. The museum's about to open! We'll just have to barge our way to the front of the queue!"

"Very un-British not to queue," remarked the Queen.

"Oh! Have you ever queued for anything in your life?"

The Queen pretended to think for a moment, before answering, to no one's surprise, "No."

"Well then, let's barge away!" said Ben.

The boy was holding the head end of the dummy, and Raj the feet. It looked like they were carrying someone who had passed out.

"So sorry!" he called to those waiting in line. "We need to come through! This lady has just fainted in the queue!"

It worked a treat. The sea of people parted. They hoisted the dummy up over their heads and made their way to the very front. They reached it just as the museum opened for the day.

"I need to see your tickets, please!" ordered the burly security guard on the door. It was the same one who'd stopped Ben when he'd found the SCRABBLE piece!

"This lady fainted!" replied Ben, affecting a high voice to match his outfit. "We need to get her sitting down!"

The security guard eyed the little princess with suspicion. "I'm sure I've seen you somewhere before, miss."

"Never been here before in my life!" Ben chirped in reply.

"And why is her dress over her face?" demanded the security guard, whisking the dress down. On revealing the face of the dummy she exclaimed, "She looks exactly like the Queen!"

Then she did a double take when she saw the real

Queen. "And so do you, Lobster Lady!" she said, studying the Queen's face. "Hang on! This is the waxwork that was stolen! Something very wrong is going on here!

I'm calling the police!"

41

"What do we do now?" asked a panicked Ben.

"Make a run for it!" said Raj.

As they spun round in panic, the dummy Queen's head bashed into the security guard's head.

CLONK!

It was a happy accident as it knocked the security guard out. She fell to the floor with a ***THUMP!***

"Let's put one back and get out of here!" hissed the Queen.

The three (well, four if you include the dummy) rushed into the museum.

"This way!" chirped the Queen.

They rushed past waxworks of pop stars, film

stars, sports stars, until they found the grand room decorated like a palace. Proudly standing there were a dozen waxworks of the royal family, all decked out in their finery.

"Where do you go?" asked Raj.

"One goes right there at the front and centre!" said the Queen proudly.

Ben and Raj put the dummy down into position.

"Ah! It's good to be back!" sighed the Queen.

Then she looked at her wet lobster costume and the clothes on the dummy. "One might just swap clothes!"

"There isn't time!" said Ben. "I can hear visitors coming into the museum right now!"

Indeed, there was the sound of excited chatter echoing along the corridors.

"One will be quick! Turn the other way, gentlemen! No peeping!"

Raj and Ben did as they were told. Then in a matter of moments the Queen called out, "You can turn round!"

Now the Queen was wearing the dummy's dress and the dummy was wearing the lobster costume.

The Queen looked like, well, *the Queen*.

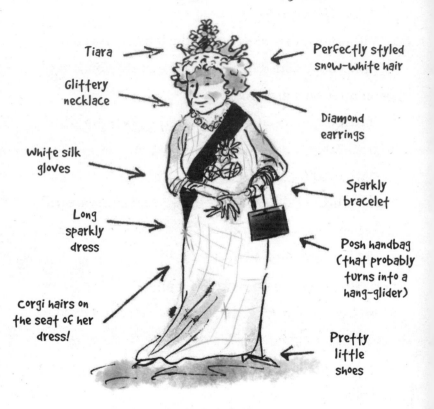

Tiara

Perfectly styled snow-white hair

Glittery necklace

Diamond earrings

White silk gloves

Sparkly bracelet

Long sparkly dress

Posh handbag (that probably turns into a hang-glider)

Corgi hairs on the seat of her dress!

Pretty little shoes

"That was quick!" remarked Ben.

"One has to be a quick dresser in this game!"

"My word!" began Raj. "My lobster costume in

Madame Tussauds! And, ma'am, may I say you look very…"

"*Queenly?*" suggested the Queen.

"Yes! *Queenly!*"

"But one rather likes one in the lobster costume."

"Me too!" said Raj, smiling. "I can do you a very good offer on a new one!"

The chatter of visitors was growing nearer and nearer.

"We need to go!" urged Ben.

The three made a run for the exit, but as they turned a corner they were met by a trio of American tourists trundling straight towards them.

"No!" exclaimed the Queen. "What are we going to do?"

"Pretend to be your own waxwork!" suggested Ben.

'What?" she spluttered.

"Just stay dead still and let us do the talking!"

For once, the Queen did as she was told, and stayed *dead still*. She didn't even blink. In moments, the American tourists, three large ladies in rain macs, jeans, sneakers and I LOVE USA T-shirts were upon them.

"Oh gee!" said one. "It's *Her Royal Majesty the Queen* of Old Merry Engerland! I need a photo to show the folks back home!"

"Me too!"

"And me!"

The three gathered around the "dummy".

"Will you kindly take the picture, please, sir?" one asked Raj.

"With pleasure, ladies!" he replied, taking the camera. "Say 'cheese'!"

"CHEESE!"

SNAP!

"She looks older than in real life!" remarked one.

"And shorter!" said another.

"And heavier!" said the third.

The Queen had been biting her lip, but she couldn't contain herself any more. "How dare you!" she thundered.

The three American ladies leaped back in fear.

"ARGH!"

"HELP!"

"IT'S ALIVE!"

"Erm… Don't worry, ladies!" said Ben. "We work here at the museum. This is just one of our new talking waxworks!"

"It's very lifelike!"

"Too lifelike!"

"Kinda spooky!"

"Well, we are just road-testing this one. Come along, robot Queen!" he said.

Together he and Raj hurried the Queen down the corridor.

"What a rude robot!" said one of the ladies.

Then the Queen turned round and blew a giant raspberry at them.

"PFFFFFFFT!"

42

"You're funny!" remarked Ben as they drove across London.

"What were you expecting of one?" asked the Queen, from behind the steering wheel.

"Well, I thought you'd be all posh and look down your nose at me and Raj."

"We're all just people, aren't we?"

"I guess so," said Ben.

"It doesn't matter what one is born into. We're all the same, really."

"But you're *the Queen!*"

"Yes, but one is much like any other old lady in Britain. I love my dogs, the odd glass of gin and watching **STRICTLY.**"

"Do all old ladies like **STRICTLY?**" asked Raj from the back seat.

"One believes so. It is the law. Especially that little heart-throb Flavio Flavioli!"

"Oh no!" cried Ben. "Not you as well!"

"Well, he is rather easy on the eye!"

Ben and Raj looked at each other, and mimed puking.

"BLEURGH!"

This amused the Queen greatly. "Ha! Ha! Ha!"

In no time, they were back at Raj's shop.

DING!

"NOOOOOOOOOOOOOOOOOO!" cried Raj as they walked through the door.

Ben had never seen him so angry. It was a scene of destruction. The floor was an ocean of sweet wrappers.

They had left PC Fudge alone there during the night, and the policeman

had managed to scoff just about everything in the shop. When they entered, he was chewing on a bar of soap!

MUNCH!

There was nothing left to eat!

"Give me that!" said Raj, snatching the half-eaten bar of soap out of the man's hand. "You can't eat this! It's soap!"

"I thought it tasted funny!" replied Fudge. "I guarded the shop well. I didn't let anyone nick a thing!"

"Well, thanks to you, there is nothing left to nick!"

"Can we all calm down now, please?" ordered the Queen. "It's very late! Fudge, it is time for you to drive one home to the palace."

"It would be an honour, ma'am!" he replied. "I will start the car." The Queen dangled the car keys in front of his face. PC Fudge took them and made his way out of the shop. "Quite a lot of what I ate was out of date," he said as he passed through the doorway.

"OUT!" yelled Raj.

DING!

PC Fudge had never moved so fast.

"Well, ma'am, I suppose this is goodbye," began Ben.

"Yes," she replied. "This has been the most **exciting** night of one's life. And, Ben, it is all thanks to you!"

"It was the most exciting night for me too. Well, let's not forget the night I had with my granny."

"No. If it wasn't for her, we would never have met, and all this would never have happened."

"She was the best."

"One knows."

"I loved her so much!" said Ben, and a tear rolled down his cheek.

The Queen embraced him, and they held each other in silence for a few moments.

"You still do love her. And you always will. When she died, you

were walking through a storm. Over time, the rain has softened, and one day one promises the sky will be blue."

"I'll never forget Granny, though!" said Ben.

"Of course you won't. She will be with you forever."

Just then something furry snaked round Ben's leg. It was the **black cat's** tail!

"PURR!"

"The **black cat!**" said the boy.

"I am sorry," said Raj. "No pets allowed in my shop!"

Ben held out his arms and the cat jumped into them. "Don't worry. I will take her home."

"PURR!"

The cat gently licked a tear from Ben's cheek.

"Thank you from the bottom of one's heart, Mr Raj," said the Queen. "I am sorry Fudge scoffed all your sweets."

"That's quite all right, ma'am."

"One will send over a huge hamper of royal goodies

for you to sell at your emporium. Honeys, jams, biscuits and the like, all from the royal estates."

Raj's face lit up with glee. "Why, thank you, ma'am!"

"You are a wonderful man, Mr Raj. We couldn't have done it without you!"

Raj lowered his head and kissed her hand.

"MWAH!"

"Farewell, chaps. One will miss you both dearly."

DING!

Ben and Raj watched the Queen walk over to the police car. She ordered Fudge to slide over into the passenger seat, and then she sat behind the steering wheel. She gave one last little royal wave before stamping her foot on the accelerator pedal…

VVVRRROOOMMM!

…and disappearing off into the distance.

"What a woman!" said Raj.

"A proper gangsta!" replied Ben. "Let me help you clear up the shop."

"Oh! You are such a good boy, Ben, but no. You

should run along home. I am sure your folks will be worried sick about you."

"They're just going to be furious with me."

"No. They are going to be so pleased to have you home safe. They love you, Ben, even if they aren't the best at showing it. And you need to introduce them to the newest member of the family. This stray cat! It obviously needs a home!"

"Oh yes. Let's see how that goes down!" replied Ben, still cradling the creature in his arms. "Goodbye, Raj!"

"Can I interest you in a very special offer on cat food?"

"I'd better go!"

"Actually, forget that! Fudge scoffed that too!"

"Ha! Ha!" laughed Ben.

Just as the boy reached the doorway, he noticed a figure outside. A figure in a pork-pie hat!

DING!

The man whisked into the shop, looking unbearably smug.

"Good morning, gentleman!" he said to Raj. "Do you have my morning newspaper? My name is… Mr Parker… or rather… **Sir Mr Parker!**"

"OH NOOOOOOOOOOOOOOO!"

cried Ben and Raj.

43

When Ben reached home, he bent down and lifted the **STRICTLY STARS DANCING** doormat to reveal the house key. It was a devilishly clever place to hide it! No robber would ever think to look there!

As soon as he put the key in the lock, he could hear voices.

"BEN!"

"BEN!"

His mum and dad were shouting his name. Were they angry with him?

Only when the boy opened the front door did he see that their faces were wet with tears.

"Oh! My little Benny!" cried Mum, hugging

him to her chest and
holding him tight.

"We were so
worried about you!"
added Dad. He came
in from behind to
make a mum-and-dad
sandwich.

"I am so sorry!"
replied Ben.

"Where have you been all night?" asked Mum.

"Well, I, er, um…"

"Go on!" prompted Dad.

"Well, I felt like I had let you down so badly in
the dance competition that I just couldn't face coming
home."

It was only half a lie. He just missed out the
tiny detail about spending all night racing around
London in a police car with Raj and *Her Majesty
the Queen.*

"*Couldn't face coming home!*" repeated Mum, now

blubbing louder than ever. "This isn't a home without you, Ben."

"You are at the centre of our world!" added Dad.

"I thought **ballroom dancing** was the centre of your world."

Mum and Dad looked at each other, uncertain of what to say.

"I would say that **ballroom** is just off-centre!" she said.

"I couldn't put it better myself!" agreed Dad.

"But is there a reason you are dressed as a princess, Ben?" asked Mum. "Is it a new dance outfit?" she added hopefully.

"No!" replied Ben firmly. "I just needed some dry clothes."

"MIAOW!" came a call from the ground.

"Whose cat is this?" asked Mum.

"It's ours," replied Ben as the cat leaped up into his arms and nuzzled against his neck.

"What's its name?" asked Dad.

Ben thought for a moment. "G. G."

"Gigi?" asked Mum.

"No! The letters G. G."

"Does it stand for something?"

"Yep!" said Ben.

"What?"

"I will tell you one day!"

"Very *mysterious!*" said Mum. "Now come on, let's get you inside."

"I'm so glad you are home, son," added Dad.

"Me too," replied Ben as they all made their way inside.

Together...

As a family.

44

THE QUEEN'S SPEECH

Only a week or so later, it was Christmas. The Herbert family, complete with G. G. the cat, or **Gangsta Granny** as Ben liked to secretly call her, sat down together to watch the Queen's speech. They

had one guest this year. Ben had suggested they invite Edna. The old lady was on her own at the old folk's home at Christmas. She didn't have any children or grandchildren, so she was delighted to be invited.

After Christmas dinner, they were all stuffed, and collapsed on to the sofa to watch the Queen's speech. Ben went bright red at seeing her again, even on the TV screen. This year, the Queen had a mischievous **glint** in her eye from the very beginning of her broadcast.

As the music of the national anthem faded out, the Queen, looking resplendent in the same dress she'd swapped with her own waxwork, addressed the nation from the ballroom of Buckingham Palace.

"As another year comes to a close, Christmas is a time for reflection," she began. "One has been reflecting oneself, on one's own life. None of us have forever, so if there is anything you have ever wanted to do, anyone you ever wanted to be, you must do it. Now. Don't wait. Recently, one had the most **thrilling** night of one's life."

From the sofa, Ben gulped, and the **black cat** sniggered.

"Hiss! Hiss! Hiss!"

"It was a night one will never forget. All you can do in this life is follow your dreams. Otherwise you're just wasting your time. In the spirit of this, one has always been glued to the television set every Saturday night to watch **STRICTLY STARS DANCING.** One has always longed to be asked to take part, but sadly one has never been asked. One doesn't know why. Is one too old? Or is one just not famous enough? Well, one doesn't care. Because right here, right now, one's Christmas present to the nation is a **ballroom** routine, assisted by the **STRICTLY** heartbreaker himself, just out of hospital where he was recovering from his broken buttock, Flavio Flavioli!"

"Jammy Queen!" exclaimed Mum.

Flavio Flavioli cha-cha-cha-ed over to the Queen and whisked her out of her seat. They danced cheek to cheek.

Ben was delighted to see his friend looking so full of joy. Who could begrudge the lady having some much-needed fun?

"Music, please!" ordered the Queen.

A military brass band in all their finery were revealed. They began a funky version of "God Save the Queen". Flavio whirled the Queen around the ballroom of Buckingham Palace. There was drama. There was comedy. There was magic. At one point, Flavio even hoisted the Queen above his head, and spun her around. People had never seen *Her Majesty* so happy! It was GLORIOUS!

As the routine ended, with the Queen draped in Flavio's arms, Ben, Mum, Dad and Edna leaped to their feet in wild applause! Even G. G. the cat put her paws together in appreciation.

A little while later, Ben and Edna were in the kitchen doing the washing-up as Mum and Dad were asleep on the sofa in front of the STRICTLY STARS DANCING *Christmas Extravaganza!* on TV.

"ZZZZ! ZZZZ! ZZZZ! ZZZZ!" they snored, missing every moment because they had eaten and drunk far too much.

"I've been thinking," began Edna.

"Oh yes?" replied Ben, handing her the gravy boat to dry.

"About what the Queen said. And did."

"It was so cool!"

"Since my husband died, I've been longing for some excitement."

"You have?"

"And I wondered if you might like to join me on a little adventure or two."

"What kind of adventure?"

"Well, all this stuff in the news about the thefts of the mask of Tutankhamun and the **WORLD CUP**."

"What of it?" asked Ben, panicked that his secret might be about to be exposed.

"The things got put back! No harm was done! It seems like the most wonderful wheeze!"

"You don't mean—?"

"I do mean. I want to be a **gangsta**, Ben. Even just for one night."

"Follow me!" said Ben.

The boy led the old lady out into the garage, the **black cat** following them.

"WOW!" cooed Edna. "She's a beauty!"

"It's Granny's old mobility scooter: **Millicent**."

"She looks so different!" marvelled Edna.

"Well, I blinged her up a bit! Made her proper **gangsta!** Fancy a ride?"

"Rather!" replied Edna, leaping into the driving seat.

Ben leaped on the back of the scooter, as G. G. jumped into the basket.

"Where shall we go?" asked Edna.

"Wherever your dreams lead you!"

"Ha! Ha!" chuckled Edna, before stamping her foot on the accelerator. "Come on, **Millicent!** Let's burn some rubber!"

VROOM!

"Here we go again!"

exclaimed Ben as they

disappeared off into the night's

adventure.

THE END...?

IF YOU HAVE ENJOYED
THIS BOOK, GO BACK TO
WHERE IT ALL BEGAN...

GANGSTA GRANNY

Meet Ben's granny.

She's very much your textbook granny:

- She smells of cabbages.
- She has used tissues tucked up her sleeve.
- And... she's an international jewel thief!

"In this gem of a book, Walliams balances high comedy with an emotional message" **Daily Mail**

"Walliams does comedy with profound, genuine heart" **Guardian**

AND, IF YOU HAVE LOVED
GANGSTA GRANNY AND THIS
GLORIOUS SEQUEL, YOU MAY
ALSO ENJOY THESE CLASSIC
DAVID WALLIAMS TITLES...

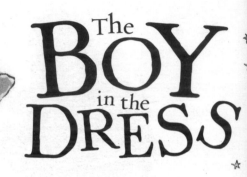

The BOY in the DRESS

Dennis lives in a boring house in a boring street in a boring town and he doesn't have much to look forward to. It was all so ordinary, something extraordinary just had to happen...

"A passionate celebration of individuality" **Telegraph**

Mr Stink

Mr Stink stank. He also stunk. And if it is correct
English to say he stinked, then he stinked as well.
He was the stinkiest stinker who ever lived.

*"A pleasure to read. A beguilingly funny, original and
thought-provoking tale... hilarious"* **The Times**